ALSO BY MELISSA BRODER

Superdoom: Selected Poems
Milk Fed
The Pisces
Last Sext
So Sad Today

Death Valley

a novel

Melissa Broder

SCRIBNER

New York   London   Toronto   Sydney   New Delhi

Scribner
An Imprint of Simon & Schuster, Inc.
1230 Avenue of the Americas
New York, NY 10020

Copyright © 2023 by Melissa Broder

SH-BOOM (LIFE COULD BE A DREAM): Words and Music by JAMES KEYES, CARL FEASTER, FLOYD MC RAE, CLAUDE FEASTER and JAMES EDWARDS. © 1954 (Renewed) UNICHAPPELL MUSIC INC. All Rights Reserved. Used by Permission of ALFRED MUSIC.

First Scribner hardcover edition October 2023

SCRIBNER and design are registered trademarks of The Gale Group, Inc., used under license by Simon & Schuster, Inc., the publisher of this work.

For information about special discounts for bulk purchases, please contact Simon & Schuster Special Sales at 1-866-506-1949 or business@simonandschuster.com.

The Simon & Schuster Speakers Bureau can bring authors to your live event. For more information or to book an event, contact the Simon & Schuster Speakers Bureau at 1-866-248-3049 or visit our website at www.simonspeakers.com.

Interior design by Yvonne Taylor

Manufactured in the United States of America

1   3   5   7   9   10   8   6   4   2

Library of Congress Control Number: 2023000945

ISBN 978-1-6680-2484-3
ISBN 978-1-6680-2489-8 (ebook)

for my father

One

I pull into the desert town at sunset feeling empty. I felt empty the whole drive from Los Angeles and hoped that my arrival would alleviate the emptiness, so when the emptiness is not alleviated, not even momentarily (all emptiness-alleviators are temporary), I feel emptier.

"Help me not be empty," I say to god in the Best Western parking lot.

Since I don't turn to god very often, I feel self-conscious when I do. I'm not sure what I'm allowed to ask for, and I worry that I shouldn't want the things I want. Are my requests too specific? I should probably ask to simply be happy doing god's will, though I've heard it said that when you're doing god's will you feel like you're flowing with a great river, not against it, so it seems like the happy feeling should just come naturally.

Earlier today, a friend texted me a quote by Kierkegaard: "Life is not a problem to be solved, but a reality to be experienced."

Ordinarily, I'd do nothing more than mark this kind of text message with a heart, maybe respond with the word *yesss*, and move on. But because of the low place I've been in, I saw the quote as a life raft, as though I were a small version of me adrift in a bowl of milk and the quote was the lone Cheerio I had to grab onto.

Halfway between LA and the desert town, I stopped at a

Circle K to pee and get some beef jerky. On the public toilet, I tried to meditate using the Kierkegaard quote as a mantra, but the quote only made me feel worse. I realized that I was doing the exact opposite of what the quote suggested: trying to solve a problem, the problem of me and my mood, rather than just experiencing it. But how do you just experience things?

In addition to the beef jerky (Jack Link's brand, Sweet & Hot) I bought a large cup of black coffee and two cans of Red Bull Sugarfree—a decision that is now coming back to haunt me in the motel parking lot. Some bad electricity is going down in my nervous system, and I can't tell what's caffeine-induced sensitivity and what could be a real physical problem. When I look at the glowing blue WELCOME sign, it appears to be vibrating.

The Best Western is at the edge of town, and beyond it lies nothingness: a desolate stretch of sand and rock, peppered with dead brush, all the way to the hills. I play it fake cool to the dust, casually unloading my black duffel from the trunk. But my hands are trembling.

Am I dying?

This thought triggers an unexpected surge of tenderness, as though I am a child who needs comforting.

In the settling dusk, I try to think of a positive self-affirmation, the kind that one woman I know has written on Post-its stuck to her bathroom mirror (a behavior that makes me judge her as a person, though there's really nothing wrong with it and I wish I didn't).

What I come up with is: *You have a good reason to be depressed.*

The phrase serves as a soothing reminder that my doominess isn't baseless. I am going to clutch it like a blankie as I move through the gloom—deeper and more alarming than my typical sea levels.

My raison de depression, if I were to convey it briefly in an e-mail, is thus:

Hi!

Five months ago, my father was critically injured in a car accident. Unfortunately, he is still in the ICU. As a result, I am overextended and cannot fulfill your request at this time.

Best,
me

One nice thing about a tragic situation is having an excuse to say no to everything. Nothing says *Don't ask me for shit* like ICU. It's simple, effective, succinct. At the same time, my prevailing compulsion is to recount every stage of the whole ordeal—as though by omission, I'll fail to convey the prolonged awfulness of the situation, or worse, I'll lose some of the time in which my father and I have existed on Earth together.

When asked, "How are you?" (never a good question) I keep bursting into monologue: his accident, his broken neck, the aspiration, the sedation, the surgery, the failure to wean off the ventilator, the prolonged unconsciousness, the tracheotomy, the awakening, the bronchoscopy and five-second death, the second death, the Decision, the really awakening, the weaning success, the collar, the sound of his voice, the pneumonia, the falling unconscious again.

Sometimes, mid-monologue, I catch myself calling my father's tracheal tube a "trach" and his ventilator a "vent"—a breezy familiarity that disgusts me, as though the life-support machines are now my friends. For the sake of narrative clarity, I do my best to organize the flood of events into temporal subheadings like Unconsciousness One and Resuscitation Two.

During the period of Unconsciousness One, my younger sister and I went to visit our father in the ICU most evenings. Through our tears we smiled at the nurses, feeling righteous and kind. What devoted children we were! What bringers of light! From our mouths burbled fountains of *I love you*s. We could not stop saying it if we tried.

We "tucked him in" each night, reading aloud from *Pat the Bunny*, *The Great Blueness*, and other bedtime classics from our faraway past. We sang "Puff the Magic Dragon" and "The Bear Went Over the Mountain," the ventilator swishing behind us for rhythm.

It is easier to have an intimate relationship with the unconscious than the conscious, the dead than the living. As my father slumbered, I created a fantasy version of him—resurrecting the man from my youth, before his depression set in. I re-entered a world of home-cooked stews, tobacco smells, cozy sweatshirts, plants, and birds; a realm of warmth and worldly cynicism, where I was always on the inside of his sarcasm.

My father is more at ease with children than with adults. At twenty-one, I was surprised to find that I could be a *them*—displaced beyond the gates of his prickly emotional garden. Now, at forty-one, I told myself a new story: if my father survived, if he awoke and had some kind of meaningful recovery, then I would have the father from my childhood back.

But I am no longer a child.

When my father regained consciousness, he wouldn't make eye contact with me. I looked at his hands and feet instead. The feet were easy: calluses, freckle on big toe, him. But looking at his left hand was like seeing him naked, like I should have to ask permission first. What was once his dominant hand—his scrawling, gardening, cooking, and hauling hand—now lay limp, with nails overgrown and skin covered in purple blotches. Gently, I took his hand in mine. He allowed me to hold it for a few seconds. Then he pulled away.

"He probably doesn't know who we are," said my sister.

But I took it personally, and in the periods of consciousness that followed, I mounted a new campaign to connect with him.

It had taken me years to see clearly that I was not the cause of my father's depression. Still, I never stopped hoping that I could be an exception to it. Now the accident was a second hurdle to overcome, and I wanted to be the magic daughter. I'd live in that garden once more.

But before I could take root, my father fell unconscious again. This time, I fled to the desert.

I'm here at the Best Western for a week under the pretext of figuring out "the desert section" of my next novel. If I'm honest, I came to escape a feeling—an attempt that's already going poorly, because unfortunately I've brought myself with me, and I see, as the last pink light creeps out to infinity, that I am still the kind of person who makes another person's coma all about me.

TWO

I chose this desert town as the scene of my escape because it's the fictional home of a cartoon bighorn sheep that enchanted both my father and me in my childhood. Whenever I see the town on a map, just north of the Mojave Preserve and south of Death Valley (in the valley of Death Valley, you might say), it makes me smile.

According to Google, the town now has two non-chain restaurants—a '50s diner and a Mexican automat—plus a Wendy's, a Jack in the Box, and other highway fare. There's a general store and trading post, an alien-themed gift shop, a small Route 66 museum, a dinosaur park, and a Target. There are five motels.

I was pleased to discover online that one of the motels is a Best Western. I love a Best Western, so much so that I'm a rewards member (though I've never earned enough points for a free night). It's an underrated motel—rivaled only by the Holiday Inn in terms of bang for your buck, plus the satisfying in-room comforts you'd find in more upscale hotels: soft sheets, fluffy towels, square lampshades. The Best Western is cozy but anonymous; simple, yet not depressing. Just about the only thing lacking is that they no longer give you the little motel notepad and pen.

Every Best Western lobby has a few unifying design rules, at least as far as I've observed, and this Best Western is no different:

Where wood can be fake, make it fake.
Where linoleum can be used, use linoleum.
If a geometric shape can be incorporated into any wall, rug, or floor tile, it's going in.

My check-in experience has the efficiency I've come to expect from a Best Western, coupled with a dash of added warmth that I find soothing, even stimulating, without being claustrophobic. This is thanks to the attention of a woman at the front desk whose name tag reads JETHRA. And Jethra is very much my type.

She is shaped like a ripe tomato. Her BEST WESTERN: BECAUSE WE CARE polo shirt exposes so much wonderful cleavage that it's hard to believe there's more breast terrain left to go beneath the shirt. But there they are. Then comes her voluptuous belly.

Jethra's fake lashes show their glue. Her nose is jolly, mouth wide. To her waist hangs a mass of hair (extensions, I think)—jet black—with half an inch of solid gray showing at the root. This I forgive her immediately, as she looks to be about my age—and I know how hard it is to keep it all together.

Using one very long pink nail as a dispatching tool, Jethra slides a small pile of forms across the fake wood counter that divides us. On her inner wrist is a tattoo with the name VIKTOR, and I wonder whether Viktor is her husband, or an ex-boyfriend, and if she could also possibly be into women (maybe it's her son).

"Now," she says. "These are your Grab N' Go breakfast bag selections sheets."

She has a throaty accent, something Eastern European-sounding.

"Make sure to fill one out every night and bring back to desk before nine p.m."

"Okay."

"Nice breakfast. I don't want you to miss."

"I won't."

"You get a choice of fruits: apple or orange. Breakfast sandwich I don't recommend. Kellogg's cereal with milk better, or bagel with cream cheese. Bagel okay, not great. I'd stick with Kellogg's. Then a yogurt. You like yogurt?"

I nod.

"Not me," she says. "I like blueberry muffin instead. It's a good muffin, if you like blueberry muffin."

"I like blueberry muffin."

"Get the muffin."

"Okay."

"Maybe you do muffin tomorrow and see how it is. If the next day you don't feel like muffin? You do granola bar."

Jethra's BECAUSE WE CARE shirt doesn't lie. She really does care. I feel warm inside—like when I get a massage or go to the gynecologist and I know the person is just doing their job, but I can't help but feel turned on by the attention.

"Room 249," she says, handing me a key card. "Down the hall and make a left. Wi-Fi password is on key slip. Indoor pool is open twenty-four hours, nice pool. You need extra towels, blanket, sheets, anything, you call desk. Do you like aliens?"

"What?"

"Do you like aliens?"

"Totally," I say, though I'm really more alien-neutral. "You?"

"I love them. We're only two hundred miles from Area 51. We get a lot of UFO-seekers; that's why I asked."

"Oh—"

"Don't forget. Grab N' Go breakfast bag selections sheets by nine."

I thank her, then make my way down the hall to my room, taking note of the ice machine and vending machines for later. I also pay close attention to the art lining the hallway walls, because this is where every Best Western establishes its individual flavor.

Best Western artworks are always photographic in medium, but the subjects chosen for representation depend on the geographic location of each motel. In this way, the art serves as little winks—reminders that we are *here*, not just in a Best Western, but in a Best Western in a *place* (in this case, the California high desert).

On my way to the room, I pass a sun-dazed mesa, a sand-dune panorama, one cowboy, two buttes, and a pack of coyotes.

Once inside the room, the desert theme continues, but with more of a "disco Negev" flavor to it. On the walls: a shiny square-and-rectangle pattern (geometric shapes)—less wallpaper than gold wall laminate. On the rug: same pattern, but make it camel. The glossy blackout curtains take a different turn with concentric circles and curlicues in shades of lime green and olive. But the whole motif comes back together with several framed close-up shots of botanic desert puffballs (healthier-looking than any desert puffballs I saw on my drive in).

It's less neutral than I'd like it. I prefer blank spaces—like I'm living on a cloud, or nowhere. Aesthetically, I feel pretty at home in my father's ICU room: the empty white walls, a single window looking out at the sky. Yesterday, the nurses even had the lights dimmed and quiet, classical music playing over a speaker system I'd never heard them use before. Spa-like.

I thought, *This is kind of nice.*

I felt envious, then immediately ashamed of the envy (who envies a man unconscious from pneumonia?), the way I do when I see this one woman nodding out on the sidewalk in front of Ralphs supermarket. Whenever I see her there, absorbed in a beatific inner world, I can't help but stare—like I'm trying to siphon off some of her heavenly high through my eyes. It's a good reminder that I'm still an addict, actually, because a normal person probably wouldn't look at this poor woman covered in sores and think, *Wow, that looks amazing.* But I see past her sores to the memory of a feeling now lost to me. I see surrender.

This is how it was for me in my father's hospital room yesterday. I wanted a sickbed of my own. I wanted to be laid out in white sheets, everything taken care of for me, and let go. Unconsciousness-envy.

I kept imagining my father saying the words, *Cool and comfortable. Cool. Comfortable.* I don't know where those words came from, but I felt as ashamed of the words as I did of the envy feeling—like it's wrong to give language to a dying man. But I couldn't stop thinking it. *Cool and comfortable. Cool. Comfortable.*

Room 249 is, if overdecorated, definitely cool and comfortable. The air-conditioning unit is already humming, set to a generous sixty-eight on the wall thermostat. I like that the bed is a king, and that there's a tiny kitchenette with a mini refrigerator, microwave, and coffee maker with little pods of coffee. It dawns on me that I feel good.

Maybe because I feel good, I give myself a doom check, and of course, the moment I do this, I don't feel good anymore. A surge of fear moves through me, and I feel my chest tighten up, heavy and tight at once, like I'm wearing a bra made of lead. I take three very deep breaths, and each one is harder to draw in. I can't tell if I'm getting enough air.

To center myself, I focus on one of the puffballs on the wall. The puffball goes psychedelic in my anxious vision, zooming in, then out. I cannot remember why I am here. It's an alien feeling (an aliens feeling?). It's a loneliness, dark blue. I came to the desert because I wanted to be alone. Now that I'm alone, it's not what I want.

I need to talk to someone. Who? I guess I have people I could call, but I can't think of anyone who won't hold me to a feeling. People are such a commitment. I would "reach out" more often if everyone promised not to check in again later. That's how they get you. Your tragedy = their ticket to texting every day. Then it becomes about their drama. It's always the people you don't want to be there for you who are there for you.

I could call a customer service representative. I have the 1-800 number for GoDaddy saved to my phone. Recently, my author website got hacked—taken over by an ad for dick pills. At first, I felt violated by the hacking. Then I forgot about it. Then the publicist who works on my books asked if I knew that my website is now an ad for dick pills. I lied and said no. She sent me a link to a $250 GoDaddy software program. It's supposed to stop bad things from happening to your website. I bought the program and installed it. Nothing happened.

I pick up my phone and immediately I'm soothed by the light of the screen. I call the 1-800 number and prepare my spiel: *dick pills, software, nothing*. A computer answers the phone. The computer welcomes me to the system. It asks me to start making choices: my customer ID, my PIN. Do I look like someone who knows her customer ID and PIN? I begin hitting the number zero repeatedly on my phone. Every time I hit zero, the computer says, "Entry not valid."

"Talk to human," I say.

"What can I help you with?" says the computer.

"Talk to human!" I say louder.

"I'm sorry, I didn't get that."

"Hu-man!"

The computer remains unfazed. But as though I have summoned him, I receive an incoming FaceTime call from my husband.

My husband is a human.

Do I want to talk to my husband?

Three

The Mexican automat is dark and loud enough for me to be totally anonymous. I enjoy eating alone in a black hole. I'm perfectly content to eat by myself in public, so long as the restaurant is crowded. There's solitude in a crowd.

This place is packed with younger, hipper LA people who came up from Joshua Tree (peasant dresses, wide-brim hats). People who call the desert "the dez." I'm wearing the same sweaty T-shirt and shorts I drove out in, plus my father's old army jacket. It still smells like him: smoke, coins, and mulch. I haven't worn it since I was a teenager, but tonight I felt like I needed the armor.

I like the automat situation: that you order by app at the table rather than interacting with an actual human. Server interactions are the prime time for any latent self-consciousness about dining solo to bubble up, and a server would push margaritas at a place like this (as a sober person, I don't need the upsell). There's a fix-ins bar, where you can help yourself to as much salsa as you want (also fortuitous, as I prefer my condiments free-flowing). On the walls are displays of saloon-kitsch ephemera: animal skulls, old license plates, a giant neon pink cactus.

I love a cactus. This is a fact I don't usually admit to because they're so popular in design nowadays, and I'd rather support an underdog. Secretly, I'd hoped to see some big ones growing wild in the desert on my drive to town. But I saw none.

Using the computer at the table, I call in my order (wet chicken burrito with extra guacamole and a Diet Coke). Then I google "cactus California" on my phone.

According to the Internet, the cacti indigenous to this area are squat little furry things with cute names like "pineapple." The one on the wall (tall with arms) is called a Saguaro, and it lives in Arizona and Mexico. There are rumored sightings of wild Saguaros growing on the California side of the Colorado River, though people on the r/botany subreddit are fighting about whether this is true.

A user named masterdon911 writes: *SAW ONE IN PALO VERDE MOUNTAINS LAST SEPT IN BLOOM AND I HAVE RECEIPTS!!!!*

To which u/pollinatr1x writes: *they don't bloom in september they bloom in may and june so screaming in all caps about cactus you obviously did not see is literally just a cry for attention*

I've gotten interested in taxonomy lately (at least enough to google "cactus California"). I'm just starting to learn about plants. I was always good with animals, but I killed every houseplant. But recently, it finally clicked that they're living things, not just decorative objects. Surprise: they really do need sunlight and water.

Now I can't stop buying them. I have to rotate plant shops out of shame (the way I used to rotate liquor stores). My house is filled with dozens of demanding young needy asshole plants. The plants are in control, not me. I'm living in a botanical orphanage.

It's also clear that I'm using the plants to try to control the uncontrollable. I wouldn't say I believe that buying just one more plant will keep my father alive (I do). But the language of plants is his language, and I want to share it.

My father knows the names of all the native Los Angeles plants—even the non-natives: Golden yarrow. Italian cyprus. Bougainvillea. Cherry laurel. Hummingbird sage. Oleander.

Bird of paradise. Jacaranda. Lemonade berry. Night-blooming jasmine. Sequoia. Spanish lavender. I still can't tell a jasmine from an oleander, but the names make me feel close to him.

I'm deep in the r/botany Saguaro conflict thread (u/convivial-katie: *Dated a hardcore saguaro-truther for 4 years and I can attest the breakup was not pleasant*) when I receive a text from my mother:

DADDY AWAKE!

I am stunned by the little gray bubble on my screen. Suddenly, everything feels very light.

My father is awake! I want to shout to the other diners, waving my phone like a torch.

But just as quickly as it came, the exuberant feeling passes. Next comes guilt. *Should I drive back to LA??* I ask my mother. *NO*, she writes. *Stay there! I don't know what's going on.*

My mother hates a change in plans. She's descended from a long line of Jewish superstitionists; bad omen experts. If you carry an umbrella: drought. If you don't: monsoon. In this case, I am the umbrella, and any sudden movements on my part will cause a reversal in my father's condition.

For our ancestors, such a jinx was corrected by intoning the Yiddish word *kinehora*: a sort-of knock-on-wood that translates to "no evil eye." But my mother puts her own spin on the *kinehora*, using the word to mean the evil eye itself, and any form of positive thinking is sure to bring the *kinehora* on. Life getting better? "No *kinehora*." Believe you have redeeming value as a human being? "Don't *kinehora* yourself."

I ask my mother if she's there at the hospital with my father. *NPpt*, she writes. *Not allowed because particle machiinw.*

I have no idea what she's talking about. I try calling her, and of course, she doesn't pick up. So I call the ICU.

The man who answers the phone has a voice like André the Giant: deep, muffled, like someone is holding a pillow over his face. He needs a translator. I've yet to ever meet André in person on the ward, but whenever I call, I get him—the ultimate gatekeeper—and only the first in a series of obstacles to reaching my father's nurse: shift changes, meal breaks, patient emergencies.

I leave my number with André and expect that I will hear back from my father's nurse sometime next year. But just as my burrito is put down in front of me, I get a video call from the hospital.

I pick up, and on the other end is a nurse I've never met before, at least as far as I can tell by her hair (purple). The rest of her is covered in something that looks like a hazmat suit. I don't ask about the suit, instead leading with a compliment about the hair (treat her like a celebrity; might need her) and then transitioning right into fact-checking my mother's statements: the consciousness, the particle machine, the not-allowed-in. Is it all true? The nurse verifies the accuracy of the report.

"He's awake and on steam inhalation," she says. "He still has antibiotic-resistant pneumonia. We can't have any visitors coming in and then spreading it to the rest of the ward."

"Oh."

"But you can talk to him if you want. Do you want to talk to him?"

The volume at the automat is rising steadily. Somebody just put "Gasolina" on the stereo.

"I do," I say.

I hear the nurse talking to my father. She sounds like she's talking to a little kid.

"You want me to hold the phone?" she asks him. "Oh, you want to hold it? Wow, look at you!"

I feel nervous. I want to say the right things to him. Perfect things. A pep talk, but not too peppy. Healing words.

My father's waxen face appears on the screen. I feel my breath catch in my throat. It isn't how skeletal he has become, or the change in his coloring, that rattle me every time I see him. It's the missing mustache. I still expect him to have his mustache.

For forty-one years, I never saw the man's upper lip. Now, they keep shaving him. I've taken to writing messages on his dry-erase board. *Dear grooming, leave mustache alone!* I tell myself I'm doing it for him, that he doesn't want to be seen without it. But he hasn't said a word about the missing mustache. He's always known what was under there: that blank stretch of skin between nose and mouth, beneath the furry patch where I assumed he began and ended. It's me who needs the mustache.

"Hello!" I say to him, too cheerfully.

Hi, he mouths back at me.

I'm taken by the simple *Hi*. I'm so taken that it might as well be a full recovery. It's a miracle *Hi*.

"Guess where I am?" I ask excitedly.

I tell him the name of the town, but he shakes his head.

"Bighorn sheep country!" I say.

No sign of recognition.

"How are you doing?" I ask.

Immediately, I regret the question. How do I think he is doing? He stares at me.

"Sorry," I say.

What? he mouths, looking annoyed.

"I was just apologizing for asking how you are doing," I tell him.

He points to his ear, and I realize it's not the question that's annoying. He can't hear me over "Gasolina."

"I'm at a Mexican automat," I say. "Mex-i-can aut-o-mat."

He shakes his head again, baffled. I realize that I have needed to cry all day.

"I'm going to let you go," I say, feeling the tears coming.

Doom is maybe just a trapped sob, I tell myself. *Remember that.*

My father nods a little, and the screen wobbles. Then his face slides out of view. All I can see is the very top of his forehead, shiny, and the catheter bag hanging overhead.

I call out a thank-you to the nurse, my voice very high, like a child's. But Nurse Purplehair must be distracted, or maybe she has left the room, because there is no response. Only the monitors, beeping.

"Thank you!" I call out again to the white ceiling.

Four

I'm getting in the car when my husband FaceTimes me again. This time, I pick up.

"Hey," he says. "Just checking to see if you're okay."

"I texted before to say I was."

"I wanted to see your face. Make sure you didn't end up on the ID channel."

Sometimes when a person who loves me expresses care, I feel oppressed. With my husband, it's like having two people hovering over me: him and his mystery illness. Tonight, his breathing is so loud that it could be a whole crowd pursuing me.

The breathing is a new symptom. The other symptoms were there from the beginning, from the onset of the flu-like illness that came over him like a tidal wave nine years ago and knocked him down beside me. When that wave receded, these symptoms remained: Persistent low-grade fever. Debilitating fatigue. Stomach cramps and diarrhea. The inability to work. The inability to walk more than a block.

Over time, I have gotten used to those symptoms (sort of). At least, I am mostly able to pretend that I have gotten used to them. I am also somewhat used to the rhythm of his waves. While there is never a full respite (he's never "well"), the illness has its own patterns. When a big wave hits, he goes down for three months in bed. These periods become more frequent every year. When we are between waves, we can do small things together like eat dinner in a restaurant, sit on the beach, go to a store. I try to be grateful for the between times.

But the breathing symptom is destabilizing in its newness, a shape-shifter. It penetrates the veil of acceptance (or feigned acceptance) I have constructed. It touches new feelings (or old feelings I wish not to feel).

On the inbreath, he makes a wet *shhh*ing sound, like he's underwater, suffocating. The inbreath is frightening. On the out-breath, he makes a fainter *ppp ppp ppp* with his lips. This sound enrages me. Then guilt. What kind of person gets angry at her husband for breathing?

"You okay?" I ask, but it comes out more accusatory than concerned.

Since my husband got sick, my words don't mean what they are supposed to mean. I can't say exactly what I'm thinking, so I use words that signify kindness as substitutes for more complex feelings. A multiplicity of meanings underlies the phrase *I love you*, which I say at least nine times a day. The phrase can mean anything from *I'm sorry you're suffering* to *Please stop talking*.

My husband nods, leans back on the pillow, and closes his eyes. I'm not sure if he's hurt by my tone, or just exhausted. I want to ask if he's okay with the way I said, *You okay?* but I don't trust how that will come out either.

I stare at him in silence. His head is getting bigger every day, swallowing up his handsome face. This is a result of the pred-nisone that his gastroenterologist put him on last year. While the steroid did nothing to help his inflamed bowels, it made his head and neck blow up like a balloon.

Sometimes, he'll be talking, and I'll envision his head lifting right off his body and sailing toward the ceiling. His mouth will be moving, but I have no idea what he's saying, because his head has taken flight. Other times, he'll rest his head on my chest and it feels like a bowling ball.

Between the weight of his head and his intense body heat, cuddling with my husband is like being buried alive in a clay oven. He takes his temperature every six hours, and it rarely dips below 99.8. I take my emotional temperature more often. I want to want my husband. It makes the not-wanting-him worse.

How can I want my husband when he's always right there? To want what you have. It's like a puzzle. But people seem to do it all the time.

"What did you do today?" I ask nervously.

It's a loaded question for a man who is a housebound invalid (his words, not mine). He opens his eyes.

"Washed your underwear," he says. "And mine."

"You didn't need to do that. Protect the envelope."

The immunologist describes my husband's body as an envelope containing a limited amount of energy. When the energy spills out, that's it.

"Nothing will ever come between me and my love of laundry," he says. "The day I can't consummate my passion is the day I'm no longer a person. Not that I'm a person now."

"You're a great person!"

"Let's change the subject," he says, letting out a sigh.

Since my father was hospitalized, my husband tries not to complain about his own prolonged health struggle. It isn't easy for an Italian American man to withhold complaints. I appreciate his efforts. But the pent-up complaints are never fully silenced. Like grinding plates, they send up shock waves from the underground in the form of wordless sighs.

He lets out a short second sigh, then a third (the notorious triple sigh), and I ask him what's wrong.

"Nothing," he says. "Why?"

We have seen twenty-seven doctors in nine years. People

believe that doctors know everything. I used to believe this. It's a very lonely feeling when the doctors can't do anything. You're calling out for help in viscid darkness, and all you get back is an echo.

A final sigh. Then: a staccato series of farts.

For years I found my husband's ass blasts amusing. I was delighted by the way that he, in return for my forgiving attitude, encouraged me to fart freely as well.

But after he got sick, the farting became more frequent. I began to feel like I was suffocating in a cloud of his flatulence; the whole house steeping in it. The scent of his farts seems to be evolving too: growing more putrid, intolerable. Can a person's farts mutate over time? Or is it only my perspective of the farts that is changing?

"You're like a farting alarm clock," I tell him.

"Oh, that's rich," he says. "Last night you detonated such a bomb in your sleep—it sounded like a duck being shot. I had to build a barricade out of pillows between you and my nose. I'm surprised you never fart yourself awake."

We laugh together. I notice that his inbreath is no longer labored; a silent inhale has replaced the *shhh*. But on the exhale, the *ppp* persists, which is strange, because never before has there been a *ppp* without a *shhh*.

I begin breathing loudly, mirroring him, hoping that this might subliminally encourage him to make an adjustment.

"I love you," I say with a mighty exhale.

"I love you and miss you," he says with a *ppp*.

Please help me to see him as You do.

This is a phrase I found in the r/beddeath subreddit provided by a user named jo_loves_frenchies as an answer to the question: *How do I become attracted to my spouse again?*

I'm wary of asking for this kind of divine help, because I'm afraid that god is going to say, *Sorry, no.* I'm rejection-sensitive;

also, impatient. If my husband doesn't immediately appear to me as a beloved child of the universe, then I am demanding too much of the universe.

Once again, it's the problem of wills (mine vs. the divine) and whether I'm allowed to ask for something so specific. I don't want to be cosmically needy. I'd rather not ask for the miracle than ask and not receive.

But as the *ppp*ing continues, it happens again:

Please help me to see him as You do.

Wandering around in the desert, there's no need to play hard to get with god.

Five

The door to my room won't open. I triple-swipe my key card, blowing on the card between swipes, but each time the light turns red, and the sensor makes a grinding noise. Rejected.

I head to the lobby in defeat. Checking in at the front desk is a fitness-y couple (smoothies, baseball caps, multitasking watches)—hikers probably, not UFO people. It's obvious they haven't been together very long, because they're performing for each other in an "opening night" sort of way, playfighting, the dude trying to take sips from the girl's smoothie and the girl laughing and batting him away.

Jethra is gone. In her place is a young man with a name tag that reads ZIP. I don't know what's with me and the Best Western staff, but Zip is very much my other type.

He is shaped like a spear of asparagus. Apart from a bulging Adam's apple (which makes me think *erection*), everything about him moves straight up and down: arms long, hands gangly. He's fumbly with his limbs, baby deer–style, like he hasn't adjusted to all his lengths yet.

His hair is less pretty: a botched attempt at bleach blond, landing on more of an orange. This I forgive him immediately, as he looks to be about twenty—and I remember how hard it is at that age to keep it all together. Even his acne (cystic, both cheeks) is attractive to me.

I pretend to be absorbed in the sign behind his head (GO. GET. REWARDED. POINTS NEVER EXPIRE) and use it as a decoy in my staring. Zip seems unaware, preoccupied with the credit card machine. But fitness girl feels my gaze. She stops playfighting, turns to face me. Her skin is luminous, flawless like a baby's. My own skin feels like parchment in the arid desert atmosphere. Clearly, I am the old woman at this party (should I have had a baby?).

When fitness girl's eyes meet mine, I quickly look away, busying myself by taking inventory of the lobby seating area: pleather sofas, big fake lollipop topiary. If my husband were with me, he'd be rising from his wheelchair while I stand in line, and I'd be saying, *Sit down! The envelope!*

It's easier to travel alone. The illness makes him so sensitive: one botched key card could drain him of everything. He's embarrassed to be using a wheelchair at fifty. Personally, the wheelchair itself bothers me least (we have fun with it, like at the supermarket, when I crash him into a cracker display and he says, *You're the worst home health care attendant ever*, and I say, *Fine, I'm quitting*, or, when the condiments aisle is too narrow for me to push him through, so he suddenly stands up out of the chair and I shout, *It's a miracle!*). At least people respect a wheelchair and don't ask dumb questions. It's a tangible symbol they can grasp onto within an otherwise-nebulous illness.

It's the trying to be present in the home for him, all that sedentary time, submerged in a whirlpool of weakness and despair and shame, that I find way heavier. I reason with him daily that it's not his fault. Why be ashamed of a condition beyond his control? I feel this way about it for him. But for myself, I do feel shame, like there is something wrong with me because he isn't well, which is maybe why it's harder to be present for my sick husband (who wants me to be present) than for my sick father (who wants to be left alone).

The fitness couple head off to their room, hauling their North Face backpacks. At last, it is my turn. Zip addresses me as "ma'am," which doesn't slow the hands of time. I report to him the situation with my key.

"Demagnetized," he says, his Adam's apple protuberant. "Happens all the time. Let me guess, you put it in your wallet with a bunch of other credit cards."

I shake my head no. I didn't put it in my wallet. But Zip is eager to give a lecture on physics and the problem of key cards in society.

"Do you know how vulnerable these are to manipulation? A hundred twenty-five kilohertz is nothing. A monkey could hack that! Somebody at the top needs to say, 'Hey! We need a mag-stripe with a higher frequency.' At least print a warning on the paper sleeve: *no wallets!*"

I liked Zip more before he started talking.

"Let me see your ID," he says. "Hold up, room 249? You haven't filled out your Grab N' Go breakfast bag selections sheet."

I tell him I forgot.

"You've got three minutes," he says, and hands me a new sheet. "Do it now."

I am unprepared for this level of intimacy.

Quickly, I check off orange juice and coffee, then the Kellogg's cereal. I find it strange that they don't specify what type of cereal (there's a real difference between Froot Loops and Rice Krispies), but I'm not about to ask Zip to elaborate.

I feel embarrassed for both of us: him for having to say the words "Grab N' Go" and me for making anticipatory breakfast choices publicly. It's a lot of humanity all at once.

In honor of Jethra, I also go with the blueberry muffin.

Six

I wake up at noon, and I'm ready to go back to sleep. When I'm not visiting my father, all I want to do is sleep. I've always loved a nap (depression), but now I have full-on performance anxiety about staying awake. No matter what I'm doing, a voice inside me is saying, *But you could be sleeping. Why not sleep instead?*

My answer to the voice is, *I am afraid that I will become nothing.*

When interviewed about my "writing process," I always say that I don't believe a person has to suffer to make art. But that's only because I imagine it's true for others (also, I don't want to be accused of inspiring teen suicide). If ever I attempt to make the inside of my skull a softer place to live (i.e., by saying kind and gentle words to myself), a counter-alert pops up inside my head that says, *This is dangerous. Do not tread here. Also, you're wrong.*

The counter-alert comes from a primal place, rooted in my survival instinct. Its message may ultimately be more destructive than helpful, but it feels like protection: self-preservation through self-flagellation. It's as though I'm wired to believe that if I say something nice to myself, cut myself any slack, it will lead to me dying.

My husband is gentle with me, the counter-voice to the counter-alert.

"You're going through a lot; you need to let yourself rest, just let yourself rest," he says.

But how can I trust him? Of course he wants me to rest, to sleep all day—don't we all want people to be like us? If we are both sleeping all the time, side by side, my husband and me, then his own depletion seems more normal to him.

"All I want," he says, "is for you to let go of your fears and worries, your self-criticism, and just relax for five minutes."

I fear we will both be sucked into the chasm of his illness, trapped there, sharing one pair of footie pajamas, no toehold, nobody to give us a leg up. I fear that I will follow him there (fall there?) only to regret having followed him—suffocation, disintegration, a dying, but no death—as I fear that I cannot follow my father (who I want to follow) where he is going.

Still, the urge to sleep all day is becoming harder to fight. Most days, I end up in a sort of no-man's-land (the Internet), where I click and scroll for hours, not writing, but not sleeping. Propelled by intermittent bursts of dopamine that punctuate my haze, I live an Internet life—one that feels like moving forward but mostly amounts to its own kind of nothing. Sometimes I wonder if I'm genuinely the introvert I think I am, or if it's just that my Internet addiction has become a substitute for needing people. Without the Internet I might be a very social person.

My third novel, the one I'm here to work on, is the story of a marriage, kind of like my marriage: the husband has a mystery illness; the doctors can't fix him; the wife is dealing with emotional fatigue (exacerbated by people asking questions for which she has no answers and prescribing podcast-y cures like "he needs to cut out wheat" and other remedies the husband tried already in a long list of ineffective remedies: rifaximin, acupuncture, dicyclomine, B-12 drip, elimination diet, amoxicillin, testosterone, probiotics, Valtrex, turmeric, fish oil, famotidine, biofeedback, Zoloft, prednisone, coffee enema, bowel rest).

Unlike my husband and me, the couple are New Yorkers who

have only been together a few years. They journey to Venice Beach in search of the California dream, which appears in the form of the young man who lives upstairs. A skater and surfer (he owns multiple boards), the young man is everything they are not—healthy, mellow, hot—and they both grow increasingly obsessed with him.

In the climax of the novel, the wife is busted stealing from Sephora (skin-care fanatic; history of acne), gets in a fight with the husband, and runs away with the skater-surfer to a music festival in the California desert, where something happens to reveal that he is not the sort of golden archangel figure she hoped he was (preferably: one who could relieve her of her own humanity) but just another boring human like the rest of us, thus demystifying both the illusion of the California dream and the value of newness, and catalyzing the kind of character transformation I'm told is necessary for a successful novel (in this case: the realization that love is not always a feeling, sometimes it's a verb, and that she loves her husband).

I don't yet know what will go down in the desert to trigger the epiphany. I'm less concerned with the inciting incident than I am with a more overarching fear that the book is too earthbound. That I am.

Before I can further grapple with such questions, I must fortify myself with a little in-room coffee (the window to pick up Grab N' Go is long past). Then I call my mother to see if she has any news about my father's condition.

"I'm worried about the sweatpants," she says.

"What?"

"The sweatpants! They've been sitting in the house for weeks."

"Oh."

Somewhere between Unconsciousness One and Unconsciousness Three, my mother's yenta friend told her that if my father was going to go to rehab after the ICU he would need multiple pairs of sweatpants. I was assigned the job of procuring the sweatpants. Unfortunately, he never made it to rehab.

"Have you heard anything from the hospital?" I ask her.

"I don't like to bother the nurses. I'll call over in a bit. I think you jumped the gun."

"What do you mean?"

"The sweatpants!"

"You told me to buy them!"

"I know," she says. "But I should have trusted my instincts and had you wait. It's like buying a gift for an unborn baby. You don't do it. Something might happen to the baby before it's born."

"So you're saying Dad got pneumonia and fell unconscious again because I bought four pairs of sweatpants on Amazon and had them shipped to your house."

"I'll just feel better if we return them."

"But he's conscious now. What if by returning them we—"

"Please."

"Fine. I'll e-mail you the return codes. Just go drop them off. You don't even have to box them up."

"I don't have to box them up?"

"No, no boxing," I say.

"Who ever heard of such a thing?"

"How are you doing otherwise? Besides the sweatpants."

"I'm fine," she says. "Why?"

Whenever I try to emotionally connect with my mother, she acts like I'm crazy to think she has feelings to express. It makes me self-conscious of my own sensitivity, like anything resembling a feeling is dramatic, frivolous, unnecessary.

People always say that it's good to feel your feelings, that if you don't feel them now, they'll come out later. But throughout this crisis, I have yet to see hers come out. And who's to say what it means to handle something well? Here I am with a full emotional range, and I'm paralyzed. Meanwhile, my mother is staying very busy with her business, the house, financial stuff. Some days I think she's headed for a fall. Most days, I feel like she's handling this well—and that her lack of an emotional response is proof that something is wrong with me.

"Oh my god!" she says. "Oh no!"

"What's wrong?!"

"Nothing," she says. "I just remembered. I have to go to Home Depot and get a hose."

Seven

I don't recommend taking a bath in a Best Western tub. Many feet have been here. Personally, I'm not afraid of germs, as I feel I've been inoculated by eating a lot of unwashed fruit, but I wouldn't advise others to do the same.

This is probably another way that I isolate myself from my fellow man: by pretending the laws of nature don't apply to me. It's like how I pretend to be at peace with the prospect of my eventual death (though not at peace with the dying process). But when I really think about it, I'm probably not okay with either.

It's only April, but the weather app on my phone says ninety-six degrees. I dress in shorts and a clean T-shirt, layering on my father's army jacket as a protective barrier against any air-conditioning I will encounter. Then I head out to find food.

In the lobby, I cast a quick glimpse over at the front desk and see that Jethra and Zip are both on duty. Zip is looking at his phone, but Jethra says hello to me, so I wave, and then I say, "Just going out for a hike!"

I don't know why I lie like this. I guess I want to seem like a woman who "does things."

"Mojave or Death Valley?" she asks.

Since I'm not actually going hiking, I don't know how to respond.

"Dunno," I say. "Just gonna see where the morning takes me!"
It's two p.m.

"Let me show you nice, easy trail close by," says Jethra.

She pulls out a piece of paper and draws on it a little map (Best Western is not the kind of place where they have maps on hand).

"Go east on highway, then north," she says, using her nail as a vector. "Will take you ten minutes."

"Twenty," says Zip, looking up from his phone for the first time.

I ignore Zip and thank Jethra directly, then head out to the car. When I step outside, the desert heat hits me like a weighted blanket. The sun is white and blazing. There's no breeze.

My car is a furnace, but at least it starts. In the console I find the remainder of yesterday's beef jerky, cooked warm, plus a hot can of Red Bull Sugarfree. Switching on the AC, I eat and drink. Then I pull out of the parking lot.

It's not until I'm a few miles down the highway that it dawns on me I'm following Jethra's map. I put on the radio and listen to a commercial for Applebee's, then the opening chords to Martha and the Vandellas' "Nowhere to Run." Quickly, I turn the radio off. This is my father's music, and it hurts too much.

I don't always avoid oldies. Sometimes I'll play his favorites on repeat—Bobby Freeman's "Do You Want to Dance" or Ritchie Valens's "Come On, Let's Go"—like pushing a wound. One night during Unconsciousness One, I watched The Young Rascals perform "Good Lovin'" on *Ed Sullivan* twenty-eight times. But I can only listen intentionally, never accidentally or casually, because the music gives me an emotional hangover.

It's the same feeling I get when I wake up from a dream that I've fallen in love with someone beautiful, only to discover that the person isn't there. My love for my father isn't romantic. But the longing has the same bereft quality. Euphoric dreams leave a question hanging in the air—the question of: *Is that all we get?*

My father's music leaves behind a similar question, only the question concerns his life: *Is that all he gets?*

Outside my window, the highway divider is strewn with trash: beer cans, a busted tire, a crumpled bedsheet, a pair of underwear (did somebody have sex on the highway?). Puffs of dry brush, like fuzzy clown wigs, grow miraculously out of cracks in the cement. They must really want to live. Or maybe I'm projecting that.

When I try to strip away my projections, I'm not left with much. I have an abundance of words for what goes on inside my brain, but they fall short when conveying nature. It's hard to describe what it is. How many times can you use the word *arid*?

But as I continue east, the landscape grows more lush. Craggy Joshua trees come howling out of the earth. There's a bounty of palm-looking things (yucca, maybe?), and brightly living shrubs in all shades of green: sea, sage, moss, chartreuse. I wish that I could drink the beauty. The emptiness is still inside me.

I search my phone for a distracting audiobook—anything but *Sweet Thursday* by John Steinbeck. Since the accident, I read all my father's favorite writers. Words don't devastate me like music, and I love inhabiting the same sentences across space and time, thinking about how he has been here. Unfortunately, the audio reader of *Sweet Thursday* keeps making a melancholic *ohhhh* sound, crooning the words "looonesome looonesome" over and over like a dirge. I can't handle a melancholic *ohhhh* right now.

I put on a new book, written by a psychic, about communicating with the dead. It's my third book on grief, death, and dying since I went on the r/deathanddying subreddit and asked: *Is it weird that I'm already mourning my father even though he's still alive?* and a user named pickleballsarah responded: *NO. It's called anticipatory grief and it's normal. LEAN IN!!!*

I kicked off my literary grief tour with a memoir by a Buddhist psychologist about his father's passing. The Buddhist psychologist mostly described how angry he felt—and how surprised he was to feel angry.

I found it strange that the Buddhist psychologist was surprised. Anger seems like a grief basic. But even more strange was the realization that I didn't feel angry. I still don't feel angry, though I wish I did, because anger seems preferable to what I've been feeling—namely fear: that the grief will paralyze me, that I'm doing something wrong, that I'll let people down, that I'm not okay. Maybe I don't have the self-esteem to feel angry.

The next book I read was a novel, described as the tale of a woman "unraveling" after the death of her wife. All I could think was, *Who unravels this neatly?* There was no mention of fear. Zero messes or catharses. If a feeling did surface, it was an elegant dribble, pristine, assonant. Was this really the inside of a person's head? I've been more unraveled by a yeast infection.

It was clear that the author had never, herself, unraveled. Also, she seemed to disapprove of humor in any form, which was another problem, because how could a person unravel so humorlessly and not die? If I saw no humor in my unraveling, I'd have been dead long ago.

The audiobook about communicating with the dead is already better than the novel was. The psychic narrates it herself, and I like her accent: New Jersey-y, real, like having Carmela Soprano for a grief counselor.

"Listen," she says. "Your dead loved ones are waiting to talk to you. So what's the holdup? Come on already! You don't need me or any other clairvoyant. You can talk to them right now! All you have to do is change your dial. Tune in to their frequency. And by 'tune in,' I mean believe!"

I like this self-starter attitude: Occult DIY. Necromantic independence. Teach a girl to fish, Carmela.

"Start asking for signs," says Carmela. "Say, 'Send me a sign to let me know you're with me.' Some of the more common signs that people report are butterflies, pennies, feathers. But don't be afraid to be specific, to ask for a specific sign. Cultivate a spirit language. Let them impress you."

I turn off the highway and head north, wondering what my father's spirit language will be. I pass a boarded-up hamburger stand and a curio shop; a gas station with only two tanks; a faded billboard for Marlboro cigarettes. Reds. My father's brand. Atop the billboard, a lone bird is perched: shiny and black, with a butter-yellow underbelly. An oriole? The bird's face and head are black, but splashed across its dark beak is another small patch of yellow—like a little mustache. Mustache oriole! A sign? But my father isn't dead. It's not him.

"I had a client whose daughter passed in childhood," says Carmela. "During our first session, she asked her daughter to send her a green apple. One green apple. An hour later I get a phone call. 'You're never going to believe this,' says my client. 'I'm at Ikea, in the kitchen section, and what do I see? A bowl of green apples! The apples are plastic, but I know it's her! She's here!'"

I can't believe this is supposed to be an encouraging story. It's terrible. A bowl of fake apples. That's all the woman has left of her daughter: a bowl of fake apples at Ikea?

"Now my client asks her daughter for apples every day," says Carmela. "She sees them everywhere! I want you to do this. Start asking for signs every day! You should be in constant communication!"

My father, living or dead, does not want to be in constant communication with anyone. There's no way I could ask him for a sign every day. What, he's trying to rest in peace, and I'm nagging him for fruit? Fruit and eternal connection? I'll definitely annoy his spirit.

If my father's spirit wants to talk to me from the afterworld, then his spirit will have to be the one that reaches out. I'm too insecure to ask anything of the dead.

Eight

At the entrance to the trail is a small, dirt parking lot, and a wooden marker with a blue dot. I leave my phone in the car; then I remember the shows my husband watches on the ID channel, how so many of the bad things that happen to women occur in the wilderness (also, in ranch-style apartment complexes, and strangely, en route to Arby's). I unlock the car, grab my phone, and I'm off.

I enter the trailhead, kicking dust, feeling better than I've felt in weeks.

My phone dings. A text from my mother: *Returned sweatpants! They said you should have gotten confirmation e-mail. Let me know!*

I tell her I'm hiking, to which she responds right away to ask if I brought water. I lie and say yes.

Hope you're not using plastic bottle, she writes. *BBAs very bad. Cancer. Saw on CNN*

Metal bottle, I write. *How is dad??*

She says he's conscious and stable. I can call him tonight.

I'm startled to discover that, while texting my mother, I've moved up the trail. I can no longer see the parking lot. I guess this is what happens when you hike (you move forward), but still I feel surprised. All around is umber rock. I have an urge to turn back, to make sure the parking lot is still behind me. Then I see

41

another trail marker, the friendly blue dot, and it makes me feel safer. My phone has all its bars. Safer still.

I know I miss a lot of life by being on my phone all the time (that's the point). But out here in nature, I feel bad about not paying attention. I decide that for the rest of the hike, I will not use the Internet or text with anyone. I'm only allowed to use my phone as a notepad to record what I see around me. I am going to notice things.

The first thing I notice is the silence. It's a full silence, a hum, as though the silence itself is an entity. It's not silence as the absence of sound, but silence as the presence of many sounds: bedrock and space, fauna and flora, all coming together to create an orchestral quiet.

I type the words, *Orchestral quiet.*

Then I observe the trees. All around are the Joshua trees, fairy-tale trees, inherently psychedelic: their twists and turns making them look like they are breathing. Of course, they are breathing, photosynthesizing, and transpiring, doing whatever it is that trees do. Ten-year-olds know how it works. I'm a slow learner.

There are other, bigger trees too: contorted-looking specimens with ashy bark and needly leaves. I want to google them, find out what they are, but a rule is a rule, no Internet, and so I make a note to do it later.

The sky is candy blue and striped with clouds. This I do not record, because I don't need it. The wife in my novel has a fear of the sky. She never looks up—not until the very end of the book (a big moment).

I'd say that her astrophobia is an aggrandized version of my own wariness of the sky—particularly the moon, which makes me feel judged (or at least ignored to an extent that its indifference feels like judgment). As a writer, there's pressure to have an intimate relationship with the moon, but the moon never seems to be putting in reciprocal effort.

Today, though, the sky strikes me as nonjudgmental. The clouds are no less indifferent than the moon, but they seem indifferent in a nicer way. Congenially neutral.

From the ground comes a faint rustling sound. Snake! No, not a snake, some kind of ashy lizard or iguana. The lizard-iguana stops. I stop. For a moment, I swear we make eye contact.

"Hey," I say to the lizard-iguana.

The lizard-iguana blinks its black eye. Its throat puffs in and out, mouth a simple line.

"I won't ask how you are doing," I say. "Or project anything on you."

The lizard-iguana scuttles off behind a boulder. I like this lizard-iguana, and I like this boulder. The lizard-iguana is doing its thing, the boulder is doing its thing, and I am doing my thing. The sun too is doing its thing. My shoulders are burning.

On either side of the trail are walls of rock (sandstone maybe?). The walls become progressively taller, creating small alleys of shade beneath them. The trees growing out of the rocks cast even bigger shadows. I begin to step from shadow to shadow to avoid the harshest of the sun's rays.

I like the way my feet feel on the trail, the crunching sound my sneakers make each time I hit the ground. I type *crunching sound*, then trip on a bush as I'm typing. I catch myself from falling by breaking into a little trot, running a few paces down the trail.

Unlike my prior cell phone–related accidents, this doesn't make me feel stupid, but is strangely exciting: a sort of adrenal-ized nowness. I am exactly where I am supposed to be, doing exactly what I am supposed to be doing. It's a rare feeling, this confidence.

I spot a jackrabbit. But it isn't a jackrabbit, just a set of sticks that look like two ears and a big rock for a body. The heat is maybe starting to get to me, because another lizard-iguana turns out to be a piece of brush.

There are plenty of bugs, though, and these are real. A pretty-looking shrub with a purple flower. More Joshua trees, more big trees, a white cloud the shape of a giant bagel. Dust and thirst. A stinging bug on my thigh. An itch. The crunch of the trail, one lone cigarette butt. *I love you, Dad.*

More dust, very thirsty now, will turn back soon. Itchy thigh, itchy vagina, a clandestine scratch. I think of Zip at the motel, wonder what his dick looks like, how big it is. Wonder if it would be weird if I went up to him and said, *Hey, I'd love to just lay around with your dick in my mouth* (it would be weird).

Another lizard-iguana, real this time. A prickly nettles thingy, so many shrubs. The walls of sandstone continuing to rise, the taste of my own sweat, Joshua trees clinging to the mountain-side, the other side a steep drop. An eroded log with a hole in it (a hole shaped like the ghost emoji). Definite weariness. The crunch, the sun, a giant cactus.

A giant cactus?

I am standing at the base of a giant cactus. It is tall, towering over me, wide too, like an elevator shaft, covering the whole width of the trail. I couldn't get my arms around it, even if I wanted to, even if it wasn't prickly, which it is, extremely, and green. The color of an olive.

It has arms, three that I can see, arching to the sky in soft U shapes—a Saguaro maybe (like the neon one at the automat, but alive).

I walk from one side of the trail to the other, examining as much of the cactus as I can. To see the whole thing, I'd have to scale the sandstone wall on the mountainside or hike down the rocks on the cliff-side (the thing is such a fatty that there's no way around it). I won't be doing either.

I try to take a pic with my phone. Every angle is too close, and I can only capture a vaguely green, shadowy swatch. Could be any cactus. Could be anything. It's like god or Ahab's whale; I can only see it in parts.

I step back and back. But the trail is too windy. My view is blocked by the big walls of rock. They seem to reach their highest point right at the cactus. I take another photo anyway. Just a sandstone blob.

I reapproach the cactus. It's got vertical ribbing, and on the raised, fleshier parts are the spikes: star-shaped clusters of them, hundreds, maybe thousands. In the sunken parts there are none; just smooth valleys, where I can touch the cactus with my whole palm and not get pricked.

The skin feels cool despite the blazing sun. But there's something tired-looking about the big vegetable, the way it leans to the right side, slumpy at the base, like it wants to recline. When I examine it more closely, I see an injury of some kind: a puncture wound, all the way from base to arms, like something slit it. It isn't bleeding. Nothing leaks from the site. But around the slit is void of spikes, only nippley calluses where the star clusters used to be, as though whatever it was that caused the injury tore them out.

I feel strangely drawn to the wound. I really want to touch it. Gently, I take one finger and trace the calluses as high as I can reach. The calluses tickle my finger beds, making me giggle. The injury looks like a pair of lips turned sideways, a peaceful, froggy almost-grin, not guffawing, but amused. I know that I am anthropomorphizing, projecting again, but it's nice to be projecting friendly qualities for once, rather than negative ones.

I imagine that I am breathing into the cactus through my fingers, healing it (though I am no healer, and probably need more repair than the cactus; *hiker, heal thyself*).

As I'm doing my healing finger-breathing, one of my fingers slips inside the slit. The cactus maintains its soft grin.

I slide my finger deeper in. It's slimy in there, cool and wet, refreshing in the parching heat. Gently, I glide my finger up and down the length of the long injury, feeling the cactus give. A second finger fits in perfectly. Then a third. Soon, I'm up to my wrist in moist flesh. It's snug, as though the cactus is giving my hand an invigorating hug, and the texture slakes my thirst, like drinking through my hand.

I make a little noise like, "Unnghhh."

I go deeper in. I find cooler, juicier flesh. The deeper I go, the wetter it gets. Then my hand hits a hard thing. I pull out a little, then back in. I circumvent the hard thing and find behind it a hollow. A smell seeps out from within. It's a bit like pumpkin, but more astringent. The white part of a watermelon? More earthen. An intoxicating smell. I want to huff it.

I wiggle my arm. The slit opens wider. Wiggle more. Wider still. I put my face up to the gap and breathe in. The gap is like a window to a pitch-dark house. I can see inside, but I can't make out anything. Wiggle wider. The gap has got to be a foot wide now. Then I stick my whole head in.

I rotate around, using my shoulders like a car jack, until I'm up to my elbows inside it. What if I run out of oxygen?

I pull back out, testing to make sure I'm still breathing. I am fine. Alive. It's actually easier to breathe inside the thing.

I feel the sun shining hot on the top of my head. I close my eyes. Then I push all the way in.

Nine

The cactus is hollow inside: a narrow chamber with a vaulted ceiling. Sun shines through the slit, illuminating the walls—the moist green flesh and latticed wooden skeleton. I keep checking the slit, touching it, to make sure I have a way out. I hope I'm not further injuring the cactus by being inside.

The ground is sand and rock, same as on the outside, with a ring of roots burrowing into the earth. I sit down on the army jacket and recline against a big rock. Looking up is like looking up inside the nave of a cathedral. What I see in that arching darkness makes me feel compelled to pray.

Instead of words, the prayer that comes out of me is a hum. I recognize the tune from somewhere; I know I didn't make it up. I keep humming until it comes to me: "Sh-Boom" by the Chords (another favorite of my father's). I close my eyes and get into it, really ham it up.

Life could be a dream. It's been days since I've prayed or meditated. *If I could take you up in paradise up above.* Unless you count the Reddit prayer or the botched Circle K toilet attempt or the botched Best Western parking lot Hail Mary. *If you would tell me I'm the only one that you love.* I don't count them. *Life could be a dream, sweetheart.* Why not? *Hello, hello again.* They weren't "successful." *Sh-boom and hopin' we'll meet again.* Does everything have to be successful? *Hey nonny ding dong.* Don't be a spiritual materialist. *Alang alang alang.* Is this song about death?

My hymn is interrupted by a scratching sound on my left. I hadn't thought about any wild animals getting into the cactus (I'd rather not be eaten, as it goes against my wish for a quick and painless death). When I open my eyes, the scratching stops. I look around. There's nothing except me and the cactus walls. I close my eyes again and get back to my *sh-boom*ing. The scratching comes back—not so much a scratching as a digging. I open my eyes and sit all the way up. There, seated next to me, playing in the sand, is a small child.

The child is a brunet with a full head of curls. A scrawny-looking thing, he wears a white T-shirt, khaki pants with big cuffs, and penny loafers. How did he get in here?

"Hello," I say.

But the child doesn't look up. He's absorbed in his playing. He has a red bucket, and beside it is a pile of stones. He is methodical: digging in the ground, sifting sand into the bucket, and then adding any stones he finds to the pile. Dig, sift, pile.

The child has small eyes, high cheekbones, and a few freckles across the bridge of his little nose. I notice that he uses his left hand for most of the action. Then I recognize the child. The child is my father.

Love floods into me: oxytocin, dopamine, sticky souls, the cleave of spirits, norepinephrine, bone and light, a covenant behind the ribs—whatever love is made of, I love this child. It's a love tinged with loss, or the anticipation of loss, the way I love my father the grown-up. To miss a person when the person is right beside you.

I want to hug the child; to feel the warmth of his scrawny body. But I'm afraid of scaring him off. So I sit very still and watch.

He turns over his bucket—one of those buckets etched with turrets and lookout holes that's used for making a sandcastle. I realize that I've seen this scene before. In an album at my parents' house, a black-and-white photo of my father as a little boy playing in the sand, same bucket. On the back of the photo, in my grandmother's handwriting: *Venice Beach 1954*. My father is five.

In the photo, he wears oversized swim shorts, no shoes or shirt. So where did these clothes come from? Another photo in the album, same summer: my father feeding seagulls on the Venice boardwalk, laughing wildly. In that photo he wears the white T-shirt, the khaki pants, the penny loafers.

My father the child lifts up his bucket. He reveals, beneath it, the perfect cylindric tower of a sandcastle.

"Very nice," I say.

This time, he turns to look at me. He gives me a little wave. He has a shy look on his face, not quite a smile, but the wave is friendly. Then he turns back to his castle.

"Do you mind if I just sit here?" I ask, extending the same question I always ask my father on hospital visits, even when he's unconscious and cannot answer (I can't help but seek approval, even when approval can't be given).

My father the child shakes his curly head no. He doesn't mind.

"You don't have to entertain me," I say, just in case he feels obligated to shake his head no when he really means, *Yes, I do mind.*

My father the child goes right on playing, dotting the turrets of his castle with stones, a hint of a smile on his face, so content to be left alone, and I see it now: he has always been a self-contained universe! To wish it otherwise is to ask him to be a different person. Not really a fair thing to ask. *Can you be other than you are?*

But I can close my eyes, opening them once in a while to make sure he is still there, until I stop opening them at all, and just listen: him digging and sifting, me breathing and *sh-boom*ing, each of us doing our thing, side by side, in parallel play, although I am not playing.

Ten

I wake up inside the cactus, ravenous. Must have drifted off. I check my phone, and it's been forty minutes. My father the child is gone.

I leave the cactus the same way I came in: out through the slit.

"I'll be back," I say, giving it a love stroke on one of its spine-less divots.

I begin the hike back to my car. After only three minutes, the way back seems longer than the way there. I keep checking my phone clock, scared that I'm lost. It's a different sort of fear than my recent doom and dread—in my gut rather than my chest—and the new fear is a reprieve from the old fear. I get why people like this outdoorsy, self-inflicted adventure stuff. There's something to be said for manufacturing a crisis (a crisis can be simpler than just living). Definitely more thrilling. Each time I see a trailmarker, I feel a flood of adrenaline.

I'm still buzzing off the cactus. My father the child: how did that happen? I don't use psychedelics. I don't even take cough medicine. Does having visions inside a cactus count as a relapse?

No, it's a sober phenomenon. A gift.

I could put the cactus in the novel. Whatever it is that needs to go down in "the desert section" could have something to do with the cactus. The inciting incident.

More action, more action, my editors are always saying. *Narrative propulsion. Raise the stakes. Something else needs to happen.*

But what really happens in life? Does anything ever actually happen?

Well. This!

Eleven

My car is in the dirt parking lot, right where I left it. No ID channel for me yet.

On the way back into town, my sister FaceTimes me. She's on with my father the grown-up. I pull off the highway onto a gravel side road that dead-ends at a small RV park. It's twilight, and I smell cooking smells: people making dinner in their mobile homes.

I thank my sister for including me on the call. We've been allies through this whole ordeal, and I'm proud of our bond. I'm always telling everyone how well we get along (mostly because it makes me feel superior to people who fight with their siblings during times of family crises; a stupid thing to compare, and not even quantifiable, as I have a nice sister, and god knows what siblings they're stuck with, but we all find reasons to feel superior to others—very pleasurable—and I'll take it where I can get it).

I hear "Purple Haze" playing in the background of my father's hospital room. He's tapping his hand in time to the music. He waves at me, and I wave back, and it means everything to me: this tapping and waving.

"Dad, are you listening to the playlist?" I ask.

"I think he is," says my sister.

The playlist is the genial capstone on the only fight we've had in five months: an iPad controversy, where my sister decided it was a good idea to buy him the device and I contested that decision.

"The man can't work an iPad when he's healthy," I told her.

"I don't want him to be bored. He needs activities."

"He's on a ventilator! Trying to breathe, that's his activity."

She smuggled the iPad in anyway. This was the night before Resuscitation One: the first of two emergencies in which my father coded blue and the hospital had to bring him back with CPR, re-injuring his ribs. I pulled the *kinehora* on my sister, blaming the Apple product for his near-death experience with a brutal "I told you so!"

I don't know why I had to be cruel. So she wanted to believe he was in good enough condition to play online solitaire. We all had our fixations (me: the mustache; my mother: getting him into the "Harvard of rehabs"). How else to channel the anxiety of the uncontrollable?

Soon, I rediverted my anxiety into making him the ultimate playlist on the iPad—all his favorites— "Peggy Sue," "Stagger Lee," "Operator," "You're Sixteen," "Get Ready," "Chain Gang," "Dance to the Music," "Sunshine of Your Love": twelve hours of music, sixteen hours of music, I didn't miss a jam. The nurses called his room "the party room." The thing was a beast; it kept growing, I couldn't stop: twenty-four hours of music, twenty-eight hours of music, B-sides, C-sides. I became a hoarder; any song from 1951–1975 was fair game. If I could just keep playlisting forever, then . . . what? I'd defeat mortality.

"Your sister made me a cassette," he said one day, pointing to the iPad.

The Stooges' "Down on the Street" was playing. Iggy Pop was yelling something about a wall.

I prepared to correct him (*No, she got you the iPad, but I'm the one who made you the "cassette"*). I wanted credit for my masterwork.

He went on, "It's supposed to be my favorite songs. But I don't know half the crap on there."

"Oh," I said, suddenly glad to be disassociated from the unhinged playlist. "She must have gotten carried away. Here, let me fix it."

I pruned way back: fourteen solid hours of only Dad-approved hits.

Now there are five of us on the call: me, my father, my sister, Jimi Hendrix, and my sister's crying baby. The baby is plump and pink. Her whole head is wet with tears. I don't know how she got tears in her little tufts of hair, but the hair is wet too. My father mouths her name over and over, makes a *shhh*ing sound.

I want the baby to stop crying, to recognize my father. But he's been in the ICU for most of her life (also, she's five months old and doesn't know shit).

I send a telepathic message to the baby: *Hey. Act like you're obsessed with him.*

My father is still *shhh*ing. The baby keeps crying.

I send more messages: *Do it for Auntie. Auntie doesn't like babies, but Auntie likes you. Oh, I know you're your own person capable of making your own decisions. No, I can't just have my own baby and use that as a weapon against my father's depression. I considered it, but even I'm not codependent enough for that.*

"All right, I'm going to go deal with her," says my sister.

She gets off the FaceTime. Then it's just me and my father. And "Ain't No Woman" by the Four Tops.

"Hi, Dad," I say.

He gives me a smile. It's a loving smile, through his small, green eyes. I forgot about that light in his eyes. I remembered the concept: my father—bringer of light—the idea of his light. But not what it actually looks like (first snow) or feels like (a fireplace).

I am glad for the light, the silence between us. It's that orchestral quiet, music and silence, both, the way the top of the ocean can be rough, while underneath it's completely serene.

His hand is still tapping (his digging hand and sifting hand). I could sit here forever (*do you mind if I just sit here?*). As long as that hand is still tapping. The light in his eyes.

My father the grown-up, my father the child. We are falling into the sunset. Falling into the night sky. Maybe the night sky is kind. Forgiving. We have both been forgiven a thousand times. Being human, always new things to forgive.

Forgive me, father.

You are already forgiven.

Forgive me, daughter.

There's nothing to forgive.

Twelve

Destiny isn't a matter of chance, it's a matter of choice, baby. Now give me some coins.

"Who's that?" asks my husband.

"Elvis. I'm at a fifties diner."

They've seated me in a sea-green booth between a case of rotating pies and an Elvis fortune-teller machine: The King Tells All (fifty cents, quarters only). It's latter-day Elvis, Vegas Elvis (bloated, sunglasses, white suit), not hot Elvis. In his rubber hands he holds a fuschia orb. Every few minutes the orb lights up and Elvis offers new wisdom:

Better to say too little than say too much and regret it later, know what I mean, baby?

On the mural wall across from me, Desi Arnaz kisses Lucille Ball. Lucy's face looks annoyed, but giant Valentine's hearts fly out of her anyway. Ricky Nelson sings "Lonesome Town" over the speakers (satellite radio, no jukebox).

"I wasn't gonna come here," I tell my husband. "Unintentional oldies."

"Walked right into the lion's den with that one."

"But, I mean, if a town has a fifties diner—"

"The diner must go off."

"Yes. Chekhov's fifties diner."

"I just ate a large ham sandwich in bed," he says.

"Provocative."

"It was highly erotic."

I was excited to tell him about the cactus, the vision I had of my father as a child. All of it. But I keep not saying it. I don't even bring up the hike. Instead, I tell him I slept all day. It's not totally a lie.

"Gustave Flaubert slept ten to twelve hours a night," he says.

"He probably didn't torture himself for depressive oversleeping."

"Au contraire," he says. "Flaubert tortured himself constantly."

I stare at the rotating pies. There's Boston cream, lemon meringue, something with an Oreo on top. The pies should go in the novel. The cactus should go in the novel. Should my father go in the novel?

"Think it was worth it?" I ask my husband.

"Worth what?"

"Worth it for Flaubert to suffer if it meant writing beautiful things?"

"Better than being the average schmo," he says. "Now the suffering is over, but the work is eternal!"

"But he isn't alive to know that."

"Eh," says my husband. "He would have been miserable either way."

Thirteen

I wake up at dawn feeling manic (good manic). To write and doubt and fear that you will fall asleep, or keep falling asleep, before you finish the thing, and then have life (or god, or something) jostle you awake and resolve the doubt and provide a path forward—this is why I write. I do it for the alchemy. I cannot just experience things. This is *how* I experience things.

So it has been decided. I, the writer, have decided. Life has decided, and overnight the decision has been crystallized: The cactus goes in the novel. My father goes in the novel.

It's simple, really: the wife has a dying father (this puts even more tension on her marriage, because in going to California, she feels she has abandoned her dying father in New York for her sick husband). Good. When the wife runs away with the skater-surfer to the music festival in the desert, she comes upon a giant cactus and, in going inside it, has a vision of her father the child, and this is the inciting incident that (somehow; still need to figure out how) triggers her character transformation (realization: love is not always a feeling, sometimes it's a verb, and that she loves her husband).

I bathe and dress quickly, eager to go see my cactus again—and hopefully, inside it, my father the child. I'm so keyed up that I don't even need coffee, but I make a little in-room cup because it's there and it's free, and I don't know how to not push an excited feeling.

Paper cup in hand, I head for the lobby. Jethra is at the front desk, and something looks different about her.

"Grab N' Go?" she asks, by way of greeting.

"Oh, shit," I say. "I forgot to fill out the form."

"It's okay, I get you one anyway," she says.

It's her lashes that have changed; they've tripled in size. Where yesterday there were two silky half-moons, today are full-on feather dusters. I don't know how she can see.

"Zip," she calls.

A door opens behind her—a black door on a black wall. I hadn't noticed the door before, and I wonder where it goes. Is it sexy back there? Loungey?

Zip pops his blond head out.

"Yeah," he says.

"She needs an extra Grab N' Go bag."

"There aren't any extras."

"Room 383 checked out last night. Give her those."

Zip disappears behind the door again, and I hear him rifling, the sound of things falling. He returns with two bags. He's looking radiant this morning—wet hair in his eyes, a little piece of lint on his Adam's apple—and I can't help but wonder: *If I could have sex with only one of them, Zip or Jethra, who would I choose?*

He hands me the Grab N' Go bags, which I grab, but I do not go, because I need more time to answer the sex question (it's challenging and requires contemplation).

"Thank you for recommending that trail yesterday," I say to Jethra.

"You liked?" she asks, using her fingernail as a toothpick to extract something from between her front teeth.

It occurs to me that I want Zip and Jethra from completely different places in my body. I want Jethra from my hips. I want

Zip from my heart. Or maybe I want Jethra from the heart and Zip from the hips.

"Loved it," I say. "I mean, the giant cactus . . . incredible."

I had not planned on saying anything to them about the cactus.

"What giant cactus?" asks Zip.

"You know," I say. "The giant cactus!"

They both look at me blankly.

"On the trail!" I say.

"I don't know giant cactus on trail," says Jethra.

"What kind of cactus was it?" asks Zip.

"Big! With arms. The one they print on everything, like at dollar stores—"

"Dollar stores?" asks Jethra.

"Like on party napkins. And folders. A Saguaro! A Saguaro cactus!"

Zip laughs smugly.

"Doubt you saw a Saguaro," he says. "They're only in the Sonoran."

"That's not true," I say. "Check Reddit."

"I've seen them in people's gardens," says Jethra.

"Yeah, people plant them. But they're not just growing in the wild."

What is he, *National Geographic*? I wish he weren't hot. Luckily, his personality is so annoying that it dispels most of the hotness. I am grateful for the dispelling.

"You seem to know a lot about cacti," I say.

"I know a few things," he says coyly. "My uncle owns Cactus Depot, a big nursery in Landers. There's no Saguaros on that trail. It was probably a Joshua tree."

"I know what a Joshua tree looks like," I say. "It wasn't a Joshua tree."

"Fine," he says. "Beavertail cactus, then."

I google *beavertail cactus*. It's a nice-looking specimen, circles and ovals, with pretty violet flowers on top. But it's not my cactus.

"Nope," I say.

"Hmmmm," says Zip. "Teddy bear cholla."

I google *teddy bear cholla*. It's a crazy-looking thing, fuzzy and flailing, more octopus than teddy bear. Definitely not my cactus.

But I feel annoyed. Also, weirdly paranoid. I wish I hadn't brought up the cactus. I don't want to talk to him about it anymore.

"Oh yes," I say. "Yep, that's it. That's what I saw. It was a teddy bear cholla."

Fourteen

I move quickly down the trail. My feet are light, flying. I feel the caffeine in my bloodstream, and the Grab N' Go bags, which I stuck in a tote along with the army jacket, tap against my hip. It's already hotter than yesterday. But inside my cactus will be cool and dark. I'll eat a picnic breakfast there—share some Froot Loops with my father the child.

I notice new things on the trail: tiny white flowers dotting the brush; a long, dried-up streambed; a piney tree, which I stop to sniff (no scent); small holes in the ground—possible tunnels for some kind of desert rodent. I even spot a beavertail cactus: flatter than the one on the Internet and crystallized, somehow. It's maybe dying. But a pretty death.

In my excitement, colors look brighter, so many shades of moss: honey gold, pistachio green, chartreuse. A bouquet of mustard-yellow flowers blooms up behind a rock. I try to pick the flowers to give to my father the child, but they fall apart in my hands.

I hunt for pretty stones instead. He can use them to decorate the turrets of his castle. I squat close to the ground, then go waddling down the trail in duck pose. I capture a pink pebble with silver flecks, a smooth, white stone (ostrich egg–esque), and a brickish shard. Each time I think I have enough I find another treasure: a terra-cotta fragment, a slate sparkler, a peach bauble. My tote gets heavier.

"Rocks," I say. "I wish I could take all of you. But I cannot. So I will conduct a brief interview. Please state, in no more than fifteen words, why you are the one to be chosen."

"Take me," says a smoke-colored globe. "I may not be the shiniest or prettiest, but I'm sturdy and stable. Also, loyal. I'll look out for you, unlike the more flamboyant stones who rely on their beauty."

"That's more than fifteen words," I say. "But okay."

I put the round rock in my tote. I imagine it smiling in there.

"Hi," says a translucent, jewel-like rectangle. "Don't I look like a sandcastle door?"

"You do," I tell it. "You're in."

More rocks erupt in chorus. Everybody wants to be chosen. But I've reached the high point of the sandstone wall, and around the next corner should be the cactus.

"I'm sorry," I say to the remaining rocks. "This is not a rejection! It's not you, it's me. I have to go see my cactus."

Standing up, I dust myself off. I feel nervous. Turning the final corner is a slow, rugged unveiling—like approaching a longed-for oasis.

Then I see green. The arms sweeping skyward. My cactus is right where I left it. My thorny phenomenon.

I scramble in closer. It's all there: the pulpy ridges, bald valleys, galaxies of spines. The cactus looks less schlumped over today than it did yesterday, but its injury seems to have worsened. At the very least, the wound has widened. Still, it's a happy-looking wound. What was yesterday a slit like a sideways smile is now a gaping guffaw of laughter.

"Hello!" I call out. "Hello, my gourd-like friend!"

The cactus laughs in silence. Unlike the rocks, I have no voice for it.

Fifteen

I climb in through the silent mouth. The cactus is still abandoned inside, no sign of my father the child anywhere: only me, my tote bag, and an atmosphere of aromatic moisture. I unpack the tote, arranging the scavenged rocks in a heart shape. I place the breakfast bags in the middle of the heart. Then I lie down on the army jacket and put my feet up on the inner skeleton.

Closing my eyes, I hum "Sh-Boom." The humming turns to singing:

Life could be a dream. Hey, Dad. *If I could take you up in paradise up above.* I miss you, Dad. *If you would tell me I'm the only one that you love.* Where are you, Dad? *Life could be a dream, sweetheart.* Come back to me. *Hello, hello again, sh-boom and hopin' we'll meet again.*

I hear the sound of an acoustic guitar. It's not "Sh-Boom," but something else. Bob Dylan. The first notes of "Girl from the North Country."

I open my eyes. Seated beside me, cross-legged, with an old-timey suitcase record player, is a boy of about thirteen or fourteen. The boy wears a black suit and a black tie. On his head is a white yarmulke and around his neck a white tallis—bar mitzvah clothes, my father's bar mitzvah clothes (the back of a photo; my grandmother's handwriting: *June 1963*).

The boy is barefoot. His eyes are closed. He is entranced by the music, swaying a little, at worship. The record player has a brown outer shell, and on the inner lid is printed in turquoise: SYMPHONIC. STEREOPHONIC. HIGH FIDELITY (my parents' attic; old suitcase record player). Bob Dylan is singing about a fair.

The boy looks over at me. He doesn't seem alarmed to see me there, lying on my back, legs up the wall. He gives me a nod, and I give him a nod in return. His cheeks are pudgy like mine were at that age (late bloomers; both of us). His hair is wiry, Brillo-y, changing (also mine).

"Cool and comfortable?" he asks.

His voice is high, my father the teen.

"Cool and comfortable," I say.

Bob Dylan is singing about a coat.

My father the teen lies down next to me on his back. He puts his legs up the wall beside mine.

"Cool and comfortable," he says again, wiggling his bare feet.

He reaches into the pocket of his suit jacket and fishes around for something. Out comes a pack of Marlboro Reds. He opens the pack, takes out a cigarette, puts it in his mouth. Then he offers me one. I accept.

"Matches?" he asks.

I shake my head no.

"Me neither," he says. "Wait a minute."

He points to the army jacket that I'm using as a blanket.

"Check the pocket," he says.

I reach into the right pocket. Nothing but crumbs and lint. I reach into the left pocket. The same.

"Inside pocket?" he asks.

I reach into the inside pocket and find an old book of cardboard matches, a plain white book. It's almost full. I rip off a match and swipe it against the sandpaper stripe. It's slow to strike. The match head crumbles against the stripe. I flip the match over and try again. This time, the match catches fire.

I light my father the teen's cigarette first. Then I light my own. The intensity of the first inhale hits me hard. I don't cough, but I get a buzz immediately. I haven't smoked a cigarette in years.

I put the matchbook back in the inner pocket of the jacket. We lie there smoking quietly, the ends of our cigarettes two orange points of light in the dark. We've smoked together before, but my father the teen doesn't say what my father the grown-up always said: *When did you start smoking? I don't believe this. Why would you start?*

And I do not say: *Years from now there will be an accident. You'll struggle to get off a ventilator. The doctors will cite your smoking as a cause of your difficulty. I'll never fault you for that, but your wife—my mother—will be angry.*

I watch the smoke go streaming up the chamber of our vessel, like incense inside a church spire. Bob Dylan is singing about being remembered.

My father the teen turns to me.

"*The Freewheelin' Bob Dylan*," he says with a smile.

He says it the way he always says it: revelatory, celebratory.

"*The Freewheelin' Bob Dylan*," I say back to him.

I say it the way I used to say it, like he says it; the way I said it before I grew up and said instead: *We're still trotting out that old horse? Hasn't enough been said about him?*

"*The Freewheelin' Bob Dylan!*" he says again.

"*The Freewheelin' Bob Dylan!*" I say, excited by what I was once excited by, then what I had the luxury of dismissing—of calling "old"—when I believed that all things would always be as they were forever, the same, never gone.

"*The Adventures of Huckleberry Finn*," says my father the teen.

I laugh at the non sequitur.

"*The Adventures of Huckleberry Finn!*" he says, more forcefully.

"*The Adventures of Huckleberry Finn!*" I say.

The song ends. I'm dizzy from my cigarette. There is a rich, staticky pause between songs, and I close my eyes to rest in the pause.

"Masters of War" comes on. But not for very long. I hear my father the teen lift the needle, skipping past the song (just as I cut off the song on a recent visit to the hospital, because, as I told my sister after, "Some songs have lyrics that are consoling to a dying man, and 'Masters of War' is not one of them").

With my eyes still closed, I wait for the opening notes of my father's favorite: "A Hard Rain's A-Gonna Fall."

But "Hard Rain" does not come. There's only more of that rich, staticky pause.

Then a wheezing sound: *heeeeeerrrrrrr*. It's a human wheeze, a person trying to catch their breath. The sound comes again: *heeeeeerrrrrrr*. It makes me shiver, a frantic, scary sound. *Heeeeeerrrrrrr, heeeeeerrrrrrr*. Faster.

I open my eyes and turn to look at my father the teen. He is calm, unchanged, still lying there, smoking in the dark. But we are not alone.

Between us stands a small boy. He is very young, cannot be more than three. His sandy hair grows in thick waves, and his skin is olive.

It's the boy who is wheezing. The horrible sounds are coming from him. He looks at me panic-stricken, and instinctively I stub out my cigarette. I sit up straight, fanning the air.

The boy tugs weakly at the straps of his little denim overalls. I notice that he wears a *Rocky* T-shirt underneath the overalls. I recognize the T-shirt from a photo (vintage Lucite family photo cube; my husband's). Then the boy coughs, and I recognize the cadence of the coughs. I'd know them anywhere. My husband's coughs. My husband the child.

My father the teen still has his cigarette lit. I tap him on the shoulder and say, "Hey!" He turns his head to look at me and

I point to the coughing toddler. But my father the teen doesn't see him.

"*The Freewheelin' Bob Dylan!*" says my father the teen.

I can't bring myself to tell him to put out his cigarette. So I beckon my husband the child closer to my side of the cactus, away from the smoke. His large brown eyes look frightened. But he forces a smile.

"Are you okay?" I whisper to him.

He nods vigorously—a tiny asthmatic boy trying to reassure me. Then, still coughing, he climbs into my lap. I hold him close and put my lips in his soft hair.

He smells like Chicken McNuggets. He smells like honey. I try my best to comfort him, making *shhhhh*ing sounds in his ear. His earlobe is pillowy and plump (my husband's earlobe).

I rock him back and forth. The rocking seems to come naturally. I don't know how I know to rock him, but I know to rock him. Gradually, his coughing subsides.

But I keep rocking. I rock and am lost in the rocking. I rock until there is nothing but my own quiet breathing. I am alone, my arms around myself, rocking.

Sixteen

When I FaceTime my husband the adult from the Wendy's parking lot, I'm still doped up on my husband the child.

"Hiiiii," I say, my voice woo-woo, pupils probably dilated.

"You really do have an overwhelming number of plants here," he says, by way of response.

Clearly, we are not on the same drug. This is the problem with human relationships: you come to a person with one feeling and they're having another.

"I watered all the plants before I left," I say. "Except Primo and Dante. Just check on them."

Primo and Dante are the two peace lilies I put in my husband's charge after a user on the r/houseplants subreddit named mebeingextraaa wrote: *caring for my ficus benjamina and watching it thrive literally healed my pre-cancerous squamous intraepithelial cervical lesions*

Unfortunately, our peace lilies are not thriving. My husband angles the phone sideways to give me a better look. Primo looks . . . not so bad, but Dante is a dismal piece of vegetation: bent stems, forlorn leaves consumed by a brown rash, a few extra-doomed fronds bleached vampire-white. Overwatered or underwatered? Nature is terrifying.

"Oh, Dante," I say.

"A real inferno."

"What should we do? Should we just toss him?"

"Toss him?"

"Yeah. I don't think it's good for morale for you to be surrounded by dying plants."

"He's not dying," he says. "He's just got—some challenges."

"He's ugly."

"So? That doesn't define him."

"You're right."

"Man. I can't believe you're giving up on Dante like that."

"I'm not giving up on Dante."

"Sure sounds that way. Heh, 'toss him.'"

"Why are you plant-shaming me?"

"I'm not shaming," he says. "I'm protecting my friend from your aesthetic judgments. Which could have real consequences for his future."

"Are you joking?"

"Not at all."

"You wouldn't even know Dante if it wasn't for me," I say.

"Doesn't mean I can't speak up for his welfare."

"I wasn't saying we should throw him in the trash. I meant out in the yard. Back to the earth."

"Maybe Dante isn't ready to go back to the earth," he says.

"How do you know what Dante is ready for? Did he tell you?"

It occurs to me that earlier today, I had a full-on conversation with a bunch of rocks. It also occurs to me that I left the rocks inside the cactus, along with the tote bag and the Grab N' Go bags (and now I'm worried the rocks are mad at me).

Still, I feel like my husband is overreaching. I don't think this is about Dante.

"Dante doesn't have to tell me how he feels," he says. "It's called empathy."

"Are you saying I lack compassion?"

"No, you're very compassionate. I'm talking about empathy."

"What's the fucking difference?"

"The difference is whether you have to identify in order to care."

"I gotta go. The hospital is FaceTiming me. With my dying father. For whom I have great empathy, even though I, myself, have never died!"

Seventeen

Nurse Purplehair is back at the helm. Except now her hair is green. She transitioned colors seamlessly.

"I've got your daughter on the phone," she says to my father. "Open your eyes."

Apparently, my father is asleep.

"He just had his eyes open one second ago," she tells me. "Maybe he's playing possum. He does that sometimes when he doesn't want to be bothered."

"I know," I say quickly, feeling self-conscious that Nurse Greenhair knows my father doesn't want to talk to me.

I remind myself that it's not personal. I remember one evening during Consciousness Two when I went in for a visit and felt certain that he was hiding from me. I said, "Hey, Dad," three times, and, when he didn't stir, I sat down on a chair at the foot of his bed to wait him out. I sat there for forty-five minutes, feeling weird, until one of the techs came in to change a bandage.

"Oh," the tech said to me. "You're here! He was really looking forward to seeing you today. Let me wake him up."

She tapped him very gently. No response. Then she said loudly in his ear, "Your daughter is here! She's come to see you!"

My father opened his eyes. He looked surprised to see me.

"Oh!" he said. "Hi, lamb."

I realized then that he really had been sleeping.

Nurse Greenhair tells me she is going to leave the phone propped up on the side table while she checks on another patient.

"Can you see him?" she asks.

I tell her I can. Then I ask her to fix my father's hospital gown where it has slipped. I don't want him to feel cold. But she is already gone, so the flimsy gown hangs off his undernourished body. I wish I could cover him. Rub his shrinking shoulders.

My father has not had a thing to eat or drink through his mouth in five months—not since his first night in the ICU, when he aspirated his dinner and they put him on a feeding tube. He told me that he dreams of Chinese food, of Jewish deli and pizza. Is he dreaming of food right now? Is he secretly awake?

"Hi, Dad," I say.

No response.

"Dad," I say. "Can you open your eyes? Just for one second? It would mean a lot to me."

Not a stir. There's only the rise and fall of his chest; the trach in his neck, its suction goggle and blue plastic tube, like a car-wash vacuum for a human being. The beeping of machines.

Shut up, I tell myself. *Leave him alone. Be like it was in the cactus with the sandcastle. Just be.*

I don't feel like a forty-one-year-old woman. I don't even feel like a *twenty*-one-year-old woman—the age I was when my bond with my father began to change, when I realized that it could change (and would change) because I'd become an adult, and he was tired, and adults, with their adult demands for intimacy, their expectations and judgments, made him more tired, and that I would be treated like any other adult—any other person— whose presence weighed more heavily on him than the small, light universe of a child.

I've been grieving the idea of my childhood father for a long time.

But I still feel like a child. Me the child. Only fatherless.

"Daddy," I say.

I'm crying.

"Daddy, look at me. I know you can. Please don't ignore me."

Let the not-dead rest, I tell myself.

It's not personal, I tell myself.

"Please, can you say you love me?"

My father opens one eye. Then he opens his other eye. He mouths something to me. But I can't understand what it is.

"I'm sorry," I tell him. "I didn't catch that."

He mouths it to me again. This time, I read his lips clearly: GO RELAX.

My father is telling me to go relax.

But I can't respond, because right then, my husband calls, and while I mean to hit the red button, I hit the green one instead.

"Hey," says my husband. "I was wrong."

"It's all right. I'm glad you protected Dante."

"No, I mean, I was wrong about *compassion* versus *empathy*. I mixed up the definitions—"

"You're calling me about etymology?"

"Yes. Are you crying?"

"I'm still on with my father. Shit! I disconnected him."

"Go," he says. "We can talk later."

"It's too late! I lost him."

"So call again."

"You think it's that easy? I have to get past André the Giant!"

"André the Giant?"

"The dude at the front desk. Don't you listen when I talk?"

I take a deep breath and try to visualize my husband the child. But all I see is my husband the child barging in on me and my father the teen.

"Why are you always interrupting?" I ask.

"Me? I'm just trying to be there for you!"

"Did I ask you to be there for me? Maybe I don't want *anyone* to be there for me!"

"Oh, really?" he says. "Well, if that's the case, I'll leave you alone, then."

"Fine," I say.

He hangs up.

Eighteen

I can't get my father back on the phone. Nurse Greenhair doesn't pick up, and André tells me a blatant lie ("five minutes").

I return to the motel with a cold Wendy's hamburger and a melting Frosty. It's nighttime, but Jethra is still at the front desk. My face is red from blubbering. I'd like to slink through the lobby without interaction, but halfway between the lollipop topiary and the random spare conference table with six chairs, she acknowledges me.

"Everything okay?" she asks.

"Yeah," I say, wiping my nose. "Guess I'm just feeling emotional that they don't give us the little Best Western notepad and pen anymore."

"What?"

"Nothing."

"You want pen?" she asks, taking a pen from a cup of pens on the desk. "Here, here is pen."

"That's okay."

"Take the pen!"

"Okay," I say. "Thanks."

I take the pen.

"My father is in the hospital," I tell her.

She exhales drowsily, as if to say, *Listen, Best Western cares, but not this much.*

But I keep talking.

"He's in the hospital in Los Angeles. He's maybe dying. I feel like I should be there, but I don't even know if he wants me there."

She nods.

"When my father was in the hospital last year, right before he died, he didn't want me there," she says.

"Your dad died?"

She nods again.

"And he wanted to be alone?"

"He didn't want me to see him like that. He was old-fashioned, Catholic Bulgarian. Very prideful dude. He was the father. He was not going to let me be the father."

"Right."

"You know about the five love languages?"

I live in LA; of course I know about the five love languages. But I shake my head no. I want to hear her tell me.

"So, people give and receive love in different ways: gifts, acts of service, physical touch, verbal, time spent."

"I think I'm verbal," I say, but she ignores me.

"My father," she says. "Not big hugger, not big talker. Acts of service, providing, putting food on table, that was his language. But in hospital, he couldn't do his language. Suddenly, I'm the one doing his language, taking care of him. And he doesn't like it. He doesn't want me to do his language. He wants to do his language! So, what, I'm expecting him to change languages? Like he is suddenly going to become physical touch language? When he is dying of all things? Pfffff, he's not going to change languages! Nobody changes languages! It's not like learning English! But I'm waiting for him to change languages. I'm waiting and waiting and it never comes."

"Wow. Did you feel guilty for being upset? That he wouldn't change languages?"

"Why guilty?"

"I don't know. I feel like something is wrong with me for being upset."

"Something *is* wrong with you. Your father is dying."

"Maybe dying. Probably."

"Your father is maybe probably dying! Of course you're upset!"

"Good point."

"That's the problem with this country," she says, motioning in the air. "All this space! No room for feeling. Have you ever been to Bulgarian funeral?"

I shake my head no.

"Oh! Well! Very different from American funeral. People are screaming, throwing dirt. People are trying to climb into the coffin!"

This is definitely better than having sex with her.

"Wow."

"Yes, I recommend. Anyway. I waited. But he never changed languages. I never got my moment. Or so I thought. But looking back, I think my father not wanting me to see him like that, weak, was his way of showing love. I thought he was trying to get rid of me. Which, yes, he was. But he was trying to protect me. Acts of service. All the way to the end. He was doing his love language."

"He was doing his love language!"

"Yep."

"Wow," I say. "Thank you."

She flutters her nails at me, like, *No big deal.*

"Do you mind if I ask . . . what was your father's name?"

"Oh," she says, smiling.

She holds up her wrist, shows me the tattoo.

"His name was Viktor," she says.

Nineteen

Back in room 249, I go on Reddit. I look up: *What is the difference between empathy and compassion?*

There are threads in dozens of subreddits devoted to the topic: r/philosophy, r/narcissism, r/stonerthoughts, r/askgaybros. Nobody is in agreement.

In the r/caregivers subreddit, a user named 1mtotalpieceofshit, writes: *Empathy is when you feel what person is feeling. Compassion is when you understand.*

WRONG, writes Cmonster22. *empathy is when you understand. compassion is when you do something about it*

Lol no, says cl3verpseudonym. *Empathy is putting yourself in other person's shoes . . . compassion is emo response.*

I text my husband:

> *Hey. I'm ready to talk etymology*
> *I'm really sorry*
> *I love you*

Then I sit down on the side of the bed and wait. It's 10:07 p.m. He's usually a very fast replier. Outside, the desert wind rattles the windows.

I check my e-mail. Somebody named Seth wants me to "lead the toast" at a virtual release party for a book of poems by a "recently deceased emerging writer." I've never heard of the writer. The book is being published posthumously by Dancing Feminist Press.

I'm sorry, I write to Seth. *Right now, I have to prioritize deaths in the order of people closest to me.*

I try calling my husband. It goes straight to voice mail.

"Hey," I say. "Can't believe we got in a fight over a peace lily."

I open the drawer to the plywood nightstand. Inside is a Gideon Bible. I take out the Bible and open it:

Are You . . . Alone, Depressed, Addicted, Stressed, Cheated, Experiencing Conflict or Temptation, Considering Suicide, Curious? Needing . . . Hope, Peace, Joy, Comfort, Purpose, Forgiveness, God?

Yeah. Obviously.

. . . If you have a personal problem concerning your relationship with God, Gideons are available to help. Please call.

I add the 1-800 number to my phone contacts as *Gideons* (because, yes, I do have a personal problem concerning my relationship with god). But I don't call. I turn to Exodus (the Bible's "desert section").

3:14 God said to Moses, I AM WHO I AM.

God using all caps like an Internet troll. Also, god is very self-accepting, it seems (mirror Post-it affirmations?). I leave the Bible on the nightstand.

By eleven p.m., I'm worried. My husband isn't the punishing type. He always responds, at least to say, *I need more time to myself.* And he never falls asleep before midnight.

I leave the room and traipse down the sage-and-rust-carpeted hallway (triangles and hexagons) to the vending machines for self-soothing candy. On the way back, I get a text from my mother: *Sweatpants got sent back to house*, she writes.

I ask her what happened. She doesn't know, but she wants me to leave the order numbers on her voice mail so she can send an angry letter to Amazon.

I'll e-mail the numbers to you and you can cut and paste, I write.

I don't know cut and paste, she replies.

I find this hard to believe. I tell her I'll walk her through it.

NO! she writes. *I don't live my life that way!!!!*

At 11:27, I open a bag of Skittles and arrange them by color on my pillow. I call my husband again. It goes to voice mail, and I hang up.

At 11:43, I eat all the reds and purples. I text him: *Can you just let me know you are okay?*

At midnight, the oranges and yellows: *Just let me know u ok*

At 12:18, the greens: *PLEASE.*

Sometime after one a.m. I text him a series of rabid question marks and then doze off. I wake up a few hours later with a Skittle (orange) stuck to my neck. I eat the Skittle and reach for my phone. No texts, but several calls: all from a number I don't recognize.

The strange number scares me. Has something bad happened to my husband? Should I go back to Los Angeles?

The calls are from GoDaddy. They want to know if I'd like to add a second software program to the $250 software program that failed to eradicate the dick pills from my website. I call the number, and a computer answers the phone. The computer welcomes me to the system.

"Hi," I say to the computer. "Should I go back to Los Angeles?"

"I'm sorry," says the computer. "I didn't get that."

"Should I go back to Los Angeles?"

"I'm sorry—"

I hang up.

I try the Gideons' number. The guy on the recording uses the phrase *team member.*

I hang up.

Awake now, I check Twitter. People on book Twitter are fighting about something. The words *trauma porn* and *centering first responders* are being thrown around.

There's also a book announcement: the sale of a new novel by a writer whose talent I admire (am jealous of). The writer is not on Twitter (also jealous of), but the announcement was tweeted earlier by her agent to much congratulatory fanfare.

The book (tentatively titled: *LOAM*) is described as:

> *The brilliantly surrealistic tale of a woman whose dead father is reincarnated as a Montezuma cypress tree (Taxodium mucronatum).*

I choke on orange-flavored spit. Dead father? Montezuma cypress tree? Brilliantly surrealistic? Taxodium mucronatum?

Do not spiral, I tell myself. *Everything is not over.*

I begin constructing mental Post-it affirmations in my mind:

> *Creativity is infinite.*
>
> *Books are in conversation all the time.*
>
> *There are enough slices of the pie for all of us (maybe).*
>
> *The only thing you can control is the work (not really).*
>
> *You are your own writer.*
>
> *Remember why you are writing this book (why?).*
>
> *A tree is different from a cactus.*
>
> *Dying is different from death.*

But is it different? How different?

Twenty

Zip is at the front desk, vaping. It's a cotton candy smell, permeating the whole lobby. When he sees me, he hides the vape pen and coughs.

"Morning," he says. "You're up early. Grab N' Go won't be ready for another two hours."

"I'm checking out."

"Right-o," he says.

"Room 249," I tell him, giving him my key card.

"Hmmm," he says, tapping on the computer. "Looks like you're booked for another three nights."

"I know," I say. "I'm going home early. Back to LA."

"Well, you'll be charged for tonight. Nothing I can do— twenty-four-hour cancellation policy. But your card will be refunded for the other two nights."

"Thanks."

"Oh. By the way. Last night . . . I went out looking for that big ol' cactus of yours. Went to the trail. Hiked out pretty far, about an hour. Brought my headlamp and a camera with me to get some photos for my uncle. The uncle with the store in Landers—"

"Right."

"Wait, lemme show you."

He opens the mystery door behind the desk and disappears inside it. When he returns, he's holding some Polaroids.

"Gotta love a real photo," he says, closing the door. "No iPhone is better than film. We really lost something as a society making that transition—"

"You got pics of the giant cactus?"

"Oh. No. I never saw it. Nope. No giant cactus. Didn't see anything higher than my knee."

"Maybe because it was dark out?"

Light or dark, there's no way to miss the cactus. It blocks the whole trail.

"Nahhhhh," he says. "I've got a monster headlamp. Fourteen hundred lumens. But I did see some really cool barrel cacti. Here, check 'em out."

He slides the Polaroids across the desk. I examine his grainy photographs. The photos are unremarkable: each featuring some squat-looking cacti from different angles.

"Nice," I say.

"Barrel cacti. You rarely see these around here. They're the drinkable ones. Like cowboys in old Westerns do it. Slice off the top, and boom: water. Of course, I'd never do that. They're protected. Don't wanna be fined."

"Right."

"Sickening how people have no respect for nature. My uncle's on the board of the National Cactus Defense League. Told me about an issue they were having near Tucson. People down there were actually shooting live rounds of bullets into Saguaro cacti! Can you believe it? Messed up! Of course, that doesn't happen here. There's nothing big enough to be worth shooting around here."

"Are you calling me a liar?"

"What?"

"About the giant cactus. Why would I lie? Why would I lie about a fucking cactus?"

"Hey, whoa, whoa, calm down. I'm not calling you anything."

The phone rings.

"Hold on," he says, and answers it. "Hello, Best Western."

I look at his dumb Polaroids on the counter.

"Yes," he says. "We have an indoor pool."

He doesn't know anything about anything.

"No, it's twenty-four hours."

Except now I'm doubting myself.

"Ten percent off for military personnel."

Am I going crazy?

"Well, thank you for your service to our country, sir."

Time to go home.

"That's about two hundred miles from here."

I pick up my duffel bag.

"I don't think anyone can promise that for certain, sir."

I head for the door.

"If you're ready to book now, I'd be happy to get you started."

I walk out.

Twenty-One

The predawn highway is dark, lit only by my high beams. Up ahead I see a small, furry creature lying dead in the road. I swerve, but not in time to miss the poor thing.

"I'm sorry," I whisper, like I'm the one who killed it.

Doom sets in. I wiggle my toes to shake off the bad adrenaline. I turn the air on, but it does nothing for my prickly sweat. Recalling an old cognitive behavioral therapy trick, I rate the feeling on a discomfort scale of one to ten (six). Then I rate my fear of the feeling (eleven).

A shred of silver light appears on the horizon. The sun. One small sliver and I'm instantly calmer. It's a good drug. And it's rising.

More colors come: a yolk of gold banded in saffron; bluish atmosphere with puffs of pink. In the new light I see mounting hills carpeted in scorched brush. Behind the hills: increscent mountains.

And I too am climbing. The glow on the glass and in my eyes. I'm not driving west toward Los Angeles. I'm headed east, into the sun, to see the cactus.

Twenty-Two

I know the sunlit trail well now—intimately, or at least, intimately enough that the blue markers no longer seem exciting (what is intimacy if not the ebb of excitement?). The familiar flora and recognizable sensations have become their own markers, and I tick off the terrain as I go along:

Parking lot and trailhead. Umber rock and orchestral quiet. The crunch of my feet, the Joshua trees. Brush, brush, and more brush.

The white flowers. The piney trees and prickly nettles. The dried-up streambed, the holes in the ground. The bugs are gone (must be sleeping).

Purple flower shrubs. Still more brush (if brush were cryptocurrency, I'd be a rich woman). Dust in my lungs (am I dying? Probably not). One lizard-iguana.

The crystallized beavertails. The rising sandstone wall and the steepening drop. Pistachio moss, chartreuse moss. Yellow flowers. Eroded ghost-emoji log.

Then the high point of the wall on the left. On the right, the steepest drop. Blind man's corner. Turn the corner. Prepare to greet the spiny mother lode!

But there is no mother lode. No succulent monolith. No vegetal column with arms reaching heavenward.

Yesterday, I am sure, a giant cactus stood here. Now there's only sand and rock. Only air. And sky.

Twenty-Three

How do you lose a giant cactus?

I pace round and round in small circles like a dog. Nothing makes sense. The rocks I collected are still here, arranged in yesterday's heart-shape formation. I imagine several of them waving with little rocky arms and giving me nice hellos, though two of them (the one that looks like an ostrich egg and the pink one with silver flecks) are snarky about having been abandoned.

"Well, well, well," says the egg rock. "Look who decided to come back."

"If it isn't Kit Carson," says the pink rock.

At the center of the rock heart is the tote containing the two Grab N' Go breakfast bags. One of the bags looks gnawed on—as though some kind of varmint got into the tote and tried its luck—but the contents are undisturbed: two bottles of water, two mini cereal boxes (Frosted Flakes; Froot Loops), two apples, two blueberry muffins.

Ostensibly, everything is exactly as I left it inside the cactus, except now there is no cactus; there aren't even the remains of a cactus: no shattered pulp, broken skeleton, or displaced thorns; no holes in the ground where roots could have been ripped out; no scars, marks, indentations. Not even any sand amiss.

"How can a thing exist and then be gone?" I ask out loud.

"How can it not?" says the translucent rock I planned to use for the castle door.

"Everything goes, sweetie," says the pink rock. "Buddhism 101."

A notification comes in on my phone. It's a text from my husband: *HEY!!* he writes. *I DROPPED MY PHONE IN THE TOILET!!! everything's fine. love you. tell me you're okay*

I feel a flood of relief. Breathlessly, I bang out a series of heart emojis. But I stop before I hit send. Then I just stand there, my thumb hovering over the phone.

"Why can't I send this?" I ask the rocks.

"Because you love power," says The Egg.

"What?"

"He scared you," says the gray rock. "He didn't mean to scare you, but he did. Now you feel angry that he scared you. You want to make him feel what you felt."

"But I should send it."

"Of course," says Gray. "Tell him where you are. Tell him you're coming home. And go home."

"No," says Pink. "Let him wait."

"I don't want to be punishing."

"Come on," says The Egg. "You love to punish."

"I don't love to punish. I just find it difficult to surrender an opportunity to punish when I've been scared."

"That's natural," says Gray. "It's frightening to love. Still, send it."

"Oh, just punish," says The Egg. "Why deprive yourself?"

"Punish him and then surprise him by coming home," says Pink.

"Or better yet, punish him and don't go home," says The Egg.

"And then what?"

"What do you mean?"

"What do I do if I don't go home?"

"Whatever you want!"

"Listen," says Door. "Punish, don't punish, punish, don't punish. How about we go look for your cactus?"

"Where?"

"Down the trail. Look. The path is clear now."

Door is right. Where the cactus blocked the way before is now wide-open terrain. I can keep going if I want.

"You think the cactus moved?"

"I don't know. It's your subjective reality."

"Seek and ye shall find," says Pink.

"Well," says Door. "Seek and ye shall seek."

Twenty-Four

I used to be a seeker. I looked everywhere for "the answer." I thought that anyone outside myself—any psychic, astrologer, healer, tarot reader—knew more than I did.

When I got sober many years ago, I stopped going to psychics (Carmela excluded). Still, I wanted a brand-name god: something totemic that I could point to, hold on to, and say, *There.* Like drugs.

Over time, that desire for a knowable god gave way to a growing sense of resignation that god was inherently unseen and untouchable, and would remain that way. I accepted that god was beyond anything that I (or anyone) could define. I became more and more surrendered to that undefinability.

When I talked about spirituality, I said things like, "If I could conceptualize god with my human mind, then how great would god be?" and "There's no need for an answer because there's nothing missing." I liked how I sounded. I thought I had it settled— settled with the unsettled. I was spiritually smug.

But I guess there is no spiritual end point, no final graduation (at least amongst the living).

Every door can be a trapdoor, every bottom a trap bottom, and my professed peace with not knowing, my answer (that no one has the answer), my arrival at a place of non-arrival, were, like so many answers and arrivals, only provisional.

Twenty-Five

I pack the four most talkative rocks into the tote: Pink, Gray, Door, and The Egg. I don't feel like talking anymore, so I bury them under the Grab N' Go stuff and my father's army jacket. Then, tote in tow, I head down the trail munching Froot Loops. I still haven't texted my husband.

It's not even eight a.m. and the heat is already ferocious. My face and neck are sticky with sweat. I swig from a liter of water, grateful to have the two smaller Best Western bottles as backup. The water is tepid, but my thirst is so intense that when it hits my tongue I feel blessed.

The terrain gets craggier; less and less trees and flora. It's prehistoric, elemental-looking, *Flinstones*-esque. I call out the word "Tectonic!" and expect to hear an echo, like I'm in the Grand Canyon. But there is no echo.

On my left, the walls of rock are rising higher, turning reddish in color. On my right, the overlook is not so steep as it was—downgraded from a cliff to a softer slope. The rocks on this side are a golden color.

I get a text from my mother:

Who is Mary Pigg-Ratliff?

I tell her that Mary Pigg-Ratliff is the big cheese at my UK

101

publisher. This makes me feel proud to have a UK publisher (then fearful again about the novel).

Well, writes my mother. *She sent wind chimes to the house. MEMORAL WIND CHIMES. With Daddy's name on them?!!!?*

Oh no. Memorial wind chimes for a living person. That's a bad *kinehora*. I try to figure out the cause of the error.

Sometime during Consciousness One (Unconsciousness Two?), my UK publicist asked me to do a last-minute interview. I declined, because my father had just coded blue that week. Twice. I think what I told the publicist was: "I'm so sorry, I can't, my father just coded."

What I guess I failed to clarify was that the doctors resuscitated him, and he survived (twice)—an error that's very unlike me, as I'm always hesitant to say things like *My father is dying* (I fear that if I tell people he's dying and he doesn't die, they will be mad at me). Still, I was under a lot of stress. How did Mary Pigg-Ratliff get my parents' address?

I'm sorry, I write. *Obviously a mistake. I'll fix. Just throw out the chimes.*

But the text won't go through.

I see that I'm down to one bar on my phone. I should probably turn around and head back to multi-bar territory. But the hike is just getting exciting. A few yards up, there's a fork in the trail.

When I get closer, I see that the fork is actually a three-pronged split: one path aiming straight ahead; one curving right—out and over the golden slope; and then another, fainter footpath, up the face of the red rock wall on my left.

If I were the fitness-y couple from the motel, I'd climb the red rock footpath, get up high enough to have a clear view of all the cacti in the area. But I'm not the fitness-y couple. I'm a center trail person, and I know this. Still, I'm intrigued by the golden slope on my right.

The path looks safe and well-trod (as though somebody

carved it clean out of the rock). It's well-thought-out: a series of horizontal passes, rather than one straight vertical climb, ramping back and forth across the face of the slope. It's like a Jacob's ladder toy folding over and over on top of itself. There's probably a good view from below.

What's even more tempting is that halfway down the slope, a succulent little something is growing. It's distinctly green and prickly, smaller than my cactus and shaped differently (like Mickey Mouse ears turned sideways; beavertail, maybe) but the first cactus I've seen in some time. Where there is one, there could be many.

I begin my descent, carefully taking the first gravelly length of the hill. It's longer than it seems. By the time I reach the cactus, six lengths down, I'm panting. I swig from the liter of water. The heat has warmed it to bath temperature through the tote. I give a few drops to the cactus as an offering. The cactus is even smaller than I thought—barely bigger than two pancakes. But it's healthy-looking and juicy. A baby?

"You're brave to be here alone," I say.

I reach out and touch a single spike with my finger (not the pointy end, but the straight needle part). It's hard as a fish bone. No subjective reality here.

"Well," I say to the fierce little thing. "Should I keep going?"

The cactus just looks at me.

On my phone I've got three bars of service. They give me courage.

Twenty-Six

A courageous heart. Could it be I have a courageous heart? Making my way across the slope path, I feel rugged. I'm a cowboy—scrappy and alive. Everything I feared before seems remote. What was I so afraid of?

I itemize my former fears, counting them on my fingers: doom, mood, magic daughter, anticipatory grief, husband illness, bed vortex, Montezuma cypress, not good enough, the sky.

With every few paces, I imagine tossing off another fear on the rugged path behind me. Fear of judgment! *Plink!* Failure! *Plank!* The erasure of all that was once familiar. *Ploonk!* Fear of relapse! *Pluff!* The fear that I've invested in foolish things (should I have had a baby?). *Plink!*

When I am out of fears (at least for now), I stop, pull down my shorts and underpants, and piss on the dust—like a courageous heart does.

"Fears, I piss on you!" I shout to the sun.

No toilet paper? No matter. A napkin from the Grab N' Go and I'm good. I stow the pissy napkin in my shorts pocket, wash my hands with a little water from the ol' liter (still a quarter tank full), and it's on with the expedition!

I eat an apple. I'm Doc Holliday. I leap a shrub. I'm Wyatt Earp. I reach the bottom of the slope path and arrive at a weedy valley, full of globe-shaped puffballs and purple blossoms. I look up, wiping the sweat from my eyes: magnificent, primeval, overpowering rock. Wild West shit. Sunlight on stone. Still no cactus.

I keep going—over and out—through a passage between two boulders, then down again (the weedy valley was a false bottom). The trail remains clear, but it's getting steeper. I slip on sand. Catch myself before I fall. Then I take it sideways. Do a little grapevine step. *Hava nagila.*

"Hey, god," I say to god.

It's easy to see god now: in the scattered blossom patches and piney trees (sparse but here). In the gold rock and amber rock. In the stacked boulders, and in the mystery of how they got stacked. In the iridescent insects: green and purple-flecked. In the water I am carrying. In my feet, which function decently. In the next little valley floor I reach.

It's a special place, this second valley. Could be a science fiction set; could be the moon. Biscuit-y sand, shadows and dunes, craterlike pits (what we talk about when we talk about the desert). Some of the pits even sparkle. I give them a closer look and find they're encrusted with a sugary, shimmering substance. Magic crystals? Or salt.

The sun has singed my shoulders red. I finish off the bottle of water and examine a small patch of Joshua trees. There are three of them, a family, maybe. Two of the trees are very tall: their crooked branches stretching wide, knifey foliage entwined. It's like they're holding hands. Or trying to stab each other. Cute and romantic. Still no cactus.

Time to head back. I tell the trees goodbye and give a few horse kicks to the glitter pits (enough to make my sneakers sparkle). But I discover a small problem. There are two paths leading out of the valley. Which path is the right one?

One path is wide. It has a gray-green boulder at its entrance. The other path is very narrow, with no other distinguishing features. I'm pretty sure the wide path is correct. But I don't remember seeing the gray-green boulder on my way here.

I turn around and position myself at the mouth of the wide path. Then I pantomime taking a few steps in. I see the crystalline pits. I see the Joshua trees on my right. Yes, the Joshua trees were on my right when I came! The wide path is correct.

I thank the trees for their assistance. Then I take the path outward. I feel confident again, back in my Wyatt Earp mindset. A cowboy doesn't panic.

Twenty-Seven

And I don't panic. Not when the trail seems strange and unfamiliar; when the rocks look whiter, bleached out, and there appear to be more ridges and ditches; when the elevation feels higher than I remember, the sun more severe, the shrubs scragglier, the way back to that first weedy valley slower; because I know that I am not a good noticer; even when I felt like I was "seeing god" on the way here I probably wasn't taking very careful notice of anything (how clearly do we ever see anything?)—the occasional piney tree, the insects, the inside of my own skull, mostly—and maybe every journey is always longer on the way back, although I would love to see one of those blue trail markers right about now, and I should probably call my husband, let him know what's happening, the plan, just in case of something.

And I don't panic. Not when I take out my phone (O warm, beloved rectangle!) and I swipe it, and the screen stays black, so I keep swiping, until finally, the phone lights up, and I call my husband's number, but it never rings, it just disconnects, and when I check the screen I see that there are no bars, only a little flag-shaped symbol where the bars should be, plus the words NO SERVICE, like a declaration of aloneness. Or nakedness.

Still, I don't panic. I just keep checking my phone every two minutes to see if the bars are back, and when the bars are not back, I return my phone to the tote and busy myself with an inventory of the other items (apple, muffins, rocks, waters, Frosted Flakes, jacket), and then a list of the colors I see around me (gold, fawn, almond, rust, sepia, mushroom, bronze, peach) before taking the phone out to check it again. And again. While the trail keeps looking stranger (I don't remember these magenta flowerlets; didn't I leave footprints?). And I can't even access a map. And when I restart my phone it does nothing to restore my service. And the phone remains a decorative object.

But I don't panic. Though it's clear that this is the wrong trail. That I should have hit the weedy valley already. That I made a mistake back at the crystalline valley, and I'll need to turn around, hike back to the crystalline valley, then take the narrow trail back to the weedy valley (and from there the golden slope to Jethra's trail, then Jethra's trail to my car, then my car to Los Angeles). I simply turn around and begin making my way back to the crystalline valley. Calmly.

A portrait of calm. This is me as I make my way back down the trail to the crystalline valley. The trail seems more familiar now that I've just taken it. I find this comforting, although I'm suspicious that it could be the right trail after all—the one I took originally on Trip One (from the weedy valley to the crystalline valley), that I simply didn't go far enough on Trip Two (from the crystalline valley to the weedy valley) to hit the weedy valley, that I turned around too soon, and am now on an erroneous Trip Three (almost-weedy valley to crystalline valley) that will then lead to an erroneous Trip Four (crystalline to not-weedy) from which I will ultimately have to turn around and take a counter-acting Trip Five (not-weedy to crystalline) and then a corrective Trip Six (this trail again) before I reach the golden slope that leads back to Jethra's trail (then Jethra's trail to my car, then my car to Los Angeles).

But my doubts are eased when, upon reaching the crystalline valley, I see the gray-green boulder at the mouth of the wide trail, and I remember that prior to departing on Trip Two, I asked myself whether I could recall seeing the gray-green boulder on Trip One, and that no, I could not recall seeing the boulder on Trip One (an instinct I should have paid attention to, and instead ignored, as I often do with instincts), but that now, seeing the boulder again after my unsuccessful Trip Two and reparative Trip Three, I can confirm that my instincts about the boulder were in fact correct, that I did not see the boulder on Trip One, and thus, the narrow trail, which I will now take on Trip Four, is the right trail.

Trip Four starts out very unpanicked, the opposite of panicked, with an almost casual elegance to it (cowboy casual), though the sun is hungry and hunting me, and I'm still checking my phone every two minutes, but in a jaunty, offhand way: yawning lazily each time to convey how easygoing I am about the whole affair.

I pop open a bottle of Best Western water and start (relaxedly) chugging away. I stop chugging for a moment when the thought comes that it's maybe a good idea to conserve water. But I start chugging again, because I don't like the thought of needing to conserve; it makes me nervous (not panicked, just nervous). I finish the bottle and wipe my mouth on my shirt (cowboy-style).

Unfortunately, this trail looks no more familiar than the other one did. The rocks are very red in color. Then I come to a fork in the trail, and this really throws me, because I don't remember a fork between weedy and crystalline. I'm not sure what to do. Do I turn around again? Keep going?

I decide that I should keep going. But I have to be strategic about it. I do an *eeny meeny miney moe*—left vs. right—and land on left. I commit to walking the left path for ten minutes. If, after ten minutes, the left path produces no weedy valley, I will come back to this fork and try right instead.

I walk the path for five minutes, timing myself on my phone

(still no service). No weedy valley. Ten minutes. No weedy anything. I decide to go just a little bit further.

Then I do come to a valley, but it's not a weedy valley. It's a rock valley. A valley at the bottom of a mountain of rock. Barren rock. Chiseled rock. Skyward-sweeping, naked rock.

It's like a hulking pile of sandstone whipping cream. Or one of the great pyramids—melting. A cosmic block. A dead end. Igneous terminus. Now I panic.

Twenty-Eight

I decide to do a (maybe) dumb thing. I abandon my plan to turn around and go back to the fork (what good is going back to the fork if I'm not even sure that the trail that led me to the fork is correct?). I will hike Rock Mountain.

I know nothing. But one thing I know is this: I need to go up. Jethra's trail is up. My car is up. Rock Mountain leads up. I can see the summit. I need a summit. Jethra's trail probably runs right through that summit. I need Jethra's trail. Up is up, isn't it?

I begin the hike. The mountain is not as steep as I thought (not even really a mountain, so much as a massive hill). I rename it Baby Rock Mountain. I take Baby Rock Mountain by storm. I go full throttle, kicking dust. Dust gets in my eyes and mouth. I cough, slipping and sliding on the loose rocks. Sweat and lotion drip down my arms and legs, making everything even slipperier. But I keep going. I feel tough. Dizzy with heat, but tough. I am on the move—making it—really making it up this fucking mountain. I'm Moses at Sinai (I'm sure Moses made some questionable decisions out of panic). I know one thing only: up.

I begin to do a little internal rhythmic chant.

Left foot. Up! Right foot. Up! Up! Up! Up! Up!

I'm panting like a feral dog. Keep going. Almost to the summit. Moses did it in sandals.

Then, as my right foot *ups*, my left foot slips. I put my hands out to catch myself from falling, but my phone is in my right hand. Hands and phone break the fall. Phone lands glass side down with a crunch. The palm of my left hand scrapes against the rocks. A stinging sensation.

I pick myself up and examine my phone first. It's badly hurt: a spiderweb cracked across the screen (still no service). Poor phone.

Then I look at my palm. It's peppered with pebbles—like I've been shrapneled. I pick out the pebbles one by one. No blood, but my flesh is pink and raw. It burns. Flakes of skin hang off like pieces of dried coconut.

It hits me then. Whatever I am doing, this is actually dangerous. Something bad could happen.

I have to get out of here.

I start up Baby Rock Mountain again. My tongue feels big in my mouth. I let it hang out. The sun is mean.

Up! Up! Up! Up! Almost there, don't stop. Up! Up! Up! Up! Moses was nuts. Up! Up! Up! Up! Left foot. Up! Right foot. Up! Up! Up! Up! Up! Summit!

Except it isn't the summit. It's a false summit: the valley of a second mountain. Not an end, but a beginning. And this second mountain is no baby. It's twice the size of the first: crusty with red earth (through what mirage or trick of distance I did not see it hovering there from below, I do not know).

I let out a wailing "Noooooo."

I hate this ugly mountain. I hate the desert. I never want to see another shrub. No more sand. And the thirst! Just get to the top. Get to the top of Red Mountain and then you can have some water.

My legs are heavy. Red Mountain is steep as hell. It's impossible—no, reframe that thinking, not impossible—challenging. Challenging and exhilarating. Exhilarating and Zen. Be one with the mountain.

"I'm sorry, mountain," I say. "I'm sorry I called you ugly. I don't hate you. I hate the situation."

No traction. Slipping and sliding. Treacherous. Slab and slab and slab.

A big penis-shaped rock looms overhead. I reach for the penis-rock to steady myself. Hands to penis-rock; almost got it. Then my ankle caves. My bum right ankle. My foot slips. This time, I fall and fall.

I fall and fall. I become an avalanche. Dust flies up as I go sliding down Red Mountain on my side. I fall for what feels like days.

I fall all the way down. I land at the fake summit. There is pain in my ankle. I am humbled. Humbled by the danger. The intensity of nature. I am humbled by the sight of my own blood.

Blood drips down my thigh. Red like the mountain. I'm bleeding on a mountain. I feel surprised. Big ugly mountain. I feel very small. Like a bug.

Or a human.

Twenty-Nine

"Is it okay to feel this much pain?" I asked my husband.

It was late one night during Unconsciousness One. I'd come home from the hospital struggling to breathe, suffocated by a thick bubble of sorrow. My husband was lying in bed. I paced back and forth by the bedside.

"Why wouldn't it be okay?" he asked.

"I don't know," I said. "I'm scared. Like it's dangerous to feel this much. Like something bad is going to happen."

"Something bad already happened," he said. "There's nothing wrong with feeling it."

"Do you ever feel pain?" I asked him.

"Ha!" he said.

It was a stupid question to ask a person who had been sick for nine years (a stupid question to ask any person).

"I mean," I said, pointing to my chest. "Right here. Heaviness."

"Every day of my life," he said.

"Really?"

I acted as if we hadn't been living together all these years, as if every one of his sighs wasn't a testament to that existential weight. Of course, I knew that he felt the heavy doom—I just wanted the comfort of shared experience.

And yet, somehow, I also didn't know?

"How do you live with it?" I asked.

"Know that it's just a moment," he said. "Don't catastrophize. Don't slap a label on it. You have to unplug the labelmaker in your brain."

It occurred to me that he was brave, my husband. It also occurred to me that he was really alive.

A living being, I thought.

"Come here," said the living being, lifting up the blanket. "Come get in."

But I was afraid.

"I'm scared," I said.

"Of me?" he asked, laughing.

"It's not safe," I said.

"Not safe? How?"

"You're going to die one day. Then what do I do? In a way, it's like you're already gone. I have to prepare."

"If that's the case, why love anyone? Everyone is going to die at some point."

"Exactly! It's like two ghosts trying to cuddle each other. Dust cuddling dust."

"Well, lucky for me, I'm going to die before you."

"You don't know that."

"It's highly likely."

"So rude," I said.

He laughed.

"Still!" I said. "It's possible. I could die before you. Then what will you do?"

He raised his dark eyebrows. His hands fell to his chest, and the blanket went fluttering down.

"See!" I said. "Dangerous!"

Thirty

I lie there for a moment on the mountain, stunned under the sky. It is an undeniably beautiful sky: cyan, with white clouds; huge, a huge sky, the same sky as everyone else's sky; always the same sky; no matter what it looks like, in any weather or any time; whatever I am doing beneath it—falling down the side of a mountain or visiting my father in the hospital—it's always the same sky. Everybody is under it.

My mother is under this sky. My sister and her baby are under this sky. My father is under this sky. My husband is under this sky.

Still, such a big aloneness.

I sit up abruptly, then make a move to stand. My right ankle caves under me, and I fall right down.

I take off my sneaker and examine the situation. My ankle is swollen—so swollen that it's the same girth as my calf. There is no bruising, but it looks bad, almost as bad as it did when I first injured it two years ago (broken tibia and acute sprain; a democracy-related injury: running to the ballot box; fell in a hole).

"Fucking idiot," I curse myself.

The blood on my scraped thigh has already begun to dry in the sun. It looks like a murder scene, but it doesn't hurt. My ankle hurts worse.

119

"Help me," I say in a whine that is almost a blubber, but not quite.

Then I do begin to blubber. I call out my husband's name, and my voice sounds hollow under the big sky. My voice sounds separate from me: the way my arm feels when I fall asleep on it and it loses feeling and it's no longer my arm for a while. This is how my voice sounds.

Then the voice that is no longer mine gets louder, more desperate. It's a shameless voice.

"Help!" yells the voice. "Heeellllp!"

I recognize the timbre of this voice: its notes of shamelessness and desperation. It is the voice of a lost person (or an actor replaying a lost person) on a show my husband watches on the ID channel, called *I Should Be Dead* or *How Am I Still Alive*, or something.

Each week, the show features the story of a different man (almost always a man, and way more outdoorsy than me) who finds himself in peril in the wilderness—he's separated from his group, or has an accident, or gets caught in a natural disaster—and the next thing you know he is clinging to a raft, or stuck between two rock faces, or trapped on a glacier.

At the very last minute, the man is always rescued. But he "should be dead."

I've seen this show three or four times, but I can't recall what any of the outdoorsy men did to help themselves be rescued. All I remember are the screams of one rugged replay actor, then a commercial for Pepcid, and then the show returning from commercial, and the narrator (deep voice-over) saying, "It's been five days, and Blake is still clinging to the glacier for dear life."

Will I be out here for five days?

I look at the clock on my shattered phone. It's just after one p.m., fewer than four hours since I arrived in the parking lot. Feels like more.

The real trouble is that no one knows I am here. Blake's wife (did Blake have a wife?) probably knew where he was going. She knew where to send the rescuers to look. And she knew where to send the rescuers to look because Blake wasn't an idiot. When Blake's wife texted him, Blake texted her back.

Wife! wrote Blake. *I am here. In the great outdoors. X marks the spot.*

And if Blake didn't have a wife, then at least he had a posse he'd traveled with who knew where he was. Or his mother knew where he was. Or the people working at the Best Western or the Holiday Inn or wherever he was staying knew where he was. Somebody knew where he was.

But nobody knows where I am. Not one person knows I am here.

Thirty-One

I try hobbling, a sort of limpy hobble, favoring my right leg. But it's too painful. Every time my right foot touches the ground, the ankle protests with a weeping pang. I try hopping on my left leg with my right leg up in the air, but the downward slope of Baby Rock Mountain is too precarious for that.

So I get down on my hands and knees. I crawl like a baby. I crawl like a baby down Baby Rock Mountain. I exclude my right hand, keeping it up behind my back, to protect my injured palm. Then I try incorporating the hand, but only the knuckle side—my fist—like a walking stick (a crawling stick). This seems to work well for a few feet. But the rocks are too hot to keep going for long.

I crawl over to the side of the slope into the shade. The air is no less hot, but the ground is cooler. I take out my last remaining water bottle, though I'm afraid to open it (if I open it I might drink it all). I leave it closed, and just lick around the outsides—the condensation that has gathered on the plastic.

I need more moisture.

I find the apple in my bag and take a huge bite. Another big bite slakes my thirst. I feel so relieved that I lean back on the cool rocks and close my eyes.

I remember how good I felt, just lying there in the hospital, after the democracy injury. My husband was in a bad health crash (he hadn't left the house in two months), so I drove myself to the ER with my left foot. I didn't even tell him I was injured until I got there.

After I checked in, they took me to an examination room, gave me a cotton gown, and told me to change and wait for the nurse. Lying on the examination table, I felt angry at first, because my husband kept texting, concerned, and his concern felt like judgment (it wasn't), an accusation that I'd done something wrong (how I interpret most things).

But after I silenced my phone, I felt better. Then I began to feel really good. I felt like a snug baby, just lying there alone on the exam table in my little cotton gown (which was surprisingly soft and comfortable). The room was warm, and the paper on the exam table made soothing crinkly sounds each time I rolled over. I began to think the words: *There is nothing to be done, nothing to be done.* I felt powerless in the best of ways.

I knew that soon, a nurse would come to take care of me, and that I would joke, *Well, I'm never voting again!* But for that soft interval, there was nothing to be done; nothing I *could* do except drift away; forced, by the gentlest of powerlessness, to drift away.

No. Do not drift away. This is not the examining table. There is no nurse coming to check in on you. Hurry up and eat the apple. Eat the apple and get out of here.

I eat the apple all the way down to the seeds. My last apple.

Then I resume the slow knuckle-crawl down Baby Rock Mountain, staying in the shade side. Every time I blink, I keep my eyes closed for what feels like a long period of time. It's as though I am losing energy through my eyes and closing them is my body's way of conserving it. Besides, I find the dark behind my lids preferable to the sunlight, and so I take the trail half-blind—feeling my way down the mountain on all fours.

My hand hits something cool and leathery and muscular. I open my eyes with a start.

Under my balled fist lies a fat snake! It's scaled brown and tan, with flecks of white. It is coiled in the shape of a pretzel.

"Sorry!" I cry out and seize back my hand.

The snake gives a little hiss (they really do hiss!) and sticks its disgusting, purple (actually forked!) tongue out at me. Then it slides off down the slope and disappears under a big rock.

Shocked, I start laughing. But I laugh too hard, and the laugh turns into a choking cough. I gasp for air in the stifling heat, and the air seems to get stuck in my windpipe—as though my breathing is suddenly voluntary.

I fear that my lungs are seizing up. Have I been poisoned by the snake?

"If you can talk you can breathe!" I say out loud, and then I keep talking to prove to myself I'm not dying.

"Venom doesn't come through a snake's skin," I say.

"It has to bite."

"How do you know it didn't bite?"

"Because it ran away."

"It wanted nothing to do with you."

"Rejected by a snake."

"You touched it nonconsensually."

"Hey, I didn't consent either!"

My dialogue is then interrupted by someone else's voice: a very low, slow, demonic voice.

"Sooometiiimes," says the voice, "people get confuuused. They're willfully confuuused. Blind to the truuuth. Afraid to see the truuuth."

Oh my god, it's the voice of Satan. The evil snake venom is inside me! But if it's the voice of Satan, then Satan has a New Jersey accent.

No, it is not the voice of Satan. It's Carmela the psychic. In all the reptilian frenzy, I must have bumped my phone and turned on the audiobook. At .5 speed.

I adjust the speed to my usual 1.5. Then I listen to Carmela for a bit as I continue to crawl my way down the mountain.

"Sometimes," says Carmela, "when I talk about signs—the apples at Ikea, or a found wedding ring, or a feather, or pennies—a client will try to get smart with me. They'll say, 'Sounds groovy, but how could my Aunt Deb's spirit be inside that penny? That penny was minted in 1982! Aunt Deb died in August.'"

Not a bad question.

"Spoiler alert!" says Carmela. "Aunt Deb is not inside the penny! Aunt Deb wasn't reincarnated as a penny. But Aunt Deb is the one who taps you on the shoulder and goes, 'Look! Look at the penny!' So that you look at the penny and you think of Aunt Deb, and you know she is still with you."

Well played, Carmela.

"And here's another thing. It isn't always Aunt Deb doing the tapping. Sometimes it's an angel, or the spirit of another loved one, or god, or any member of your luminous entourage—"

My luminous entourage?

"—your luminous entourage tapping you on the shoulder and saying, 'Look at the penny!' So that you look at the penny and you think of Aunt Deb, and you know she is still with you. Because your luminous entourage wants you to know that you're not alone. And sooner or later, folks, you gotta face it: you've got a whole luminous entourage working on your behalf."

I find this improbable. Also, strangely comforting.

On the one hand, Carmela probably has the term *luminous entourage* trademarked and is working on the rollout of a candle line for Target. And yet, if her theory is correct, it's a possible answer to a question I've had throughout my father's health crisis, which is: Why do I feel, at times, like he is already speaking to me from beyond the grave? There are those phrases I hear in my mind. *Cool and comfortable* is one. Another is: *Yes, my angel.*

Carmela would probably say that I'm right: those phrases

aren't coming from me, but they're not necessarily coming from my not-dead father, from not-beyond the grave. They are coming from my "luminous entourage." The entourage is trying to let me know—something.

"Just remember," says Carmela. "Aunt Deb may be working in cahoots with your luminous entourage. But she ain't the whole posse."

My phone battery is down to 22 percent. I turn off Carmela.

Thirty-Two

I make it all the way down Baby Rock Mountain on my hands and knees. When I reach Rock Valley, I kiss a big red rock.

Rock Valley turns out to be an easier crawl than Baby Rock Mountain (namely because it's flat), and I get through fairly quickly (a twelve-minute crawl) and uneventfully (no snakes) to the mouth of the path that led me there. At the mouth of the path, I kiss the sand.

Still down on all fours, I head down the path. My morale is now, while not great, better, and I hum little snatches of "The Bear Went Over the Mountain" through sandy lips. But when I get to the fork in the path, things go awry.

Here is a little lesson in outdoorsmanship: If a path forks into two paths, and each of the paths (the initial path and the two forking paths) are the same width, with the same characteristics (rocks, sand, shrubs; because you're in a fucking desert), and you're the type of person who has never once remembered where she parked a car—a person who always texts herself a reminder at the mall (parking spot, garage floor, and nearest elevator if possible)—then do yourself a favor and, when confronted with a fork on a desert path, text yourself a brief note like:

Hi! Hope you don't have to return to this fork. But, if you do, here are some simple instructions on how to determine which of the three identical-looking paths (initial path and two forking paths) to take back. P.S. Try not to fall down any mountains.

I texted myself no such note. And I am in trouble. Big trouble. I have no idea which direction to go. I need help; real help. Where is my luminous entourage? I also really need water.

I fumble around in the tote for the last Best Western water bottle. My hand hits something hard and fragmented. The rocks! Yes! I will ask them which way to go. They are of the earth and will connect me to the earth (I too am of the earth, but disconnected).

When all four rocks are in my palm and accounted for (Pink, Gray, The Egg, and Door), I prepare to issue my plea. But first they have to chide me.

"Well, well, well," says The Egg. "Look who decided to grace us with airtime."

"If it isn't Calamity Jane," says Pink.

"Knock it off," I tell them. "I need help."

"Hmmm," says The Egg. "What's it worth to you?"

"Yeah, what do we get in return?" asks Pink.

"Remember," says Door. "Not all those who wander—"

"Hey!" I say to Door. "Now's not the time for your dorm-room philosophy. You're the one who got me into this mess."

The Egg snickers at Door.

"*All* of you," I say to The Egg.

Only Gray says nothing. I can tell that he (he seems like a he) is holding himself back, not saying the obvious thing, which is, *I told you to just text your husband and go home.*

"What do you think?" I ask Gray.

Gray is silent for a moment (arguably, he's silent for eternity, depending on one's views of sentience and inanimate objects found in nature, but I am lost and desperate, and do not have the luxury of debating geological consciousness).

"Left," says Gray quietly. "Let's try left."

Thirty-Three

I don't know if there is such a thing as "officially lost," or what makes a person maybe lost vs. sort of lost vs. *lost*. There were times in my life when I felt totally lost and then realized I was only sort of lost, or not lost at all. There were other times when I felt not-lost and later realized I was completely lost. Most of these were emotional.

But if there is such a thing as "officially lost," a confirming factor of lostness, a certification or blue check mark that verifies one's lost status, I now have the check mark. Gray was wrong. The left path was wrong. I am lost.

I must now think like a lost person. I have to view the world through a lost person's eyes. I have to make preparations.

My biggest problem is water. I've got a single bottle left and a constant thirst. I keep taking out the bottle and staring at it, holding it up to my eye, turning the landscape into a blur and the light into a prismatic rainbow (as though I can imbibe the water osmotically through my eye).

I want to gulp the whole thing, but I need to ration. The bottle is conveniently divvied into sections: ringed by thirteen equidistant circular divets. One ring section = approximately two sips. I will allow myself no more than one ring section per hour.

My other biggest problem is that nobody knows I'm here. Nobody even knows I am missing. Even if they knew where to

131

look for me, they don't know *to* look for me. Why would they? My husband thinks I'm at the Best Western, being punishing. The question then is just how big of an asshole he believes I'm capable of being. How long does he think I intend to go on ignoring him?

Historically, I've never been a skilled ignorer. I can't remember ever ignoring him for more than, let's say, six hours. Still, it would be quite the leap to presume me missing based on a few non-responses, no matter how much ID channel he watches (a lot). I imagine he won't construct any full-on doomsday scenarios until at least twenty-four hours have passed since my last text. My last text was at 1:09 this morning (the rabid question marks).

Then there is the question of what he will do with his concerns. The practical next move would be to check in with my mother and ask her if she has heard from me, but knowing their dynamic (she does not do well with his illness; too much humanity), he'll want to postpone this communication as long as possible. He certainly won't text her at 1:09 a.m. I think the earliest he'd reach out would be tomorrow after ten a.m. when he wakes up.

There is also the possibility that my mother will keep texting me about the wind chimes and/or the sweatpants (or, less likely, about something having to do with the real crisis at hand: my father). Upon not hearing back from me, she'll grow impatient and call my husband, probably tomorrow, to ask him what's going on. But even if the two of them, upon confirming that neither has heard from me in twenty-four hours, are plunged into a torrent of worry—what then?

Do they call the Best Western? Probably. But let's say they do call (sometime tomorrow) and they find out that I checked out this morning, do they alert the authorities? Who are the authorities? Am I "missing enough" to commence a search? And where do they search?

I imagine the authorities will first want to talk to Jethra and Zip.

Jethra will say, *The last time I saw her, I taught her the five love languages.*

The authorities will write down: *Five love languages.*

Zip will say, *When she checked out, she said she was going back to Los Angeles.*

Then the authorities will search west of the Best Western—between the motel and Los Angeles. They will not search here. Because where is here?

Some path. Some path in some desert in some life. And this is the part of the life where I am lost in the desert. But the world is round and covered in oceans. So why am I here?

I'm here because I put myself here. Or because I was put here? Because I am supposed to be here? Because New Age jargon.

Because my father. Because illness. Because my husband. Because avoidance.

Because nature. Because man vs. nature. Because I'm not supposed to be here? Because hubris.

Because a novel. Because I was lost to begin with. Because everything we love we will lose. I am here because a cactus.

Thirty-Four

Helllp! Hello?! Help me! Helllp!

More yelling. Me yelling. There are only so many variations on *help*, and I use them all. I am crawling, yelling, and crying. I don't want to cry (can't afford to lose the water), but I can't stop. I've become a baby. In a basin. The wrong path has led me to some kind of wrong basin (a very dry, wrong basin). Scorched earth, zero hydration. It's like a thousand-year drought, a baked lake, the size of a baseball field and bordered by mountains.

My tears water the basin. They do not caulk the fissures. There are cracks everywhere: the ground webbed in them, labyrinthine, the ghosts of no-rain past. They give me the creeps; electric shivers down my sunburnt skin. They're like grooves on a dusty brain. Like the earth is trying to think but can't. I can't either.

Good. Don't think. Use animal instinct. Pretend you are an animal. What kind of animal? I feel like a bug. In a basin. A dry drain.

It's heavy to be a bug. Much heavier than I'd imagine. Why do I feel so heavy? Antennae? Wings? Self-pity?

Self-pity. Un-bug-like. And not an earned feeling. After all, I'm the one who got myself into this mess. Still. Self-pity, punctuated by self-blame (Elisabeth Kübler-Ross's five stages of something? Dehydration?).

I think of my father. Livid after his accident. When he could finally speak, he blamed himself.

"So stupid!" he said. "I really messed up!"

"They call it an accident because it's an accident," I said. "If it wasn't an accident, they wouldn't call it an accident."

I was repeating something that his father, my grandfather, once said to me.

"So stupid!" he said again.

Behind the anger, I think, was self-pity. The feeling of being very small. Less frightening to be angry and not feel so small. Some sense of control in that. Less like a bug in a basin.

I am going to die out here. I might. I could. Die. All this time I should have been practicing for dying. What was I doing instead? Reading reviews of sweatpants. For hours.

But how do you practice for dying?

Monks do it. You have to devote your life to it like they devote their lives (and even they're not ready). Every bug in line. Into the fissures.

It's brave of us to die! I know we have no choice, but that doesn't make it less brave. How tenderly I feel for all of us when I think of this. It makes me want to give up gossip forever. If I get out of the desert alive, I'll do my best.

How do you do it, Dad? How do you die?

He doesn't know either.

I have watched him at funerals. It seemed far off, that he would. Die. Later, later, there would be time for that later. He was immunized by time. And if he was immune, then I was extra-immune. Graveside, we stood there like winners. And the one in the ground had lost. But the win was temporary, and time was speeding up. Everybody into the ground. Everybody already in the ground.

No, animals don't think these things. Be like the desert hare. Better yet, be a mountain lion.

What does the injured mountain lion do? She licks her wounds. What else? She tries to conserve her energy. Yes, and how? I don't know, something involving her cubs. She makes her cubs do something.

But what about the childless injured mountain lion? How does the childless injured mountain lion conserve energy?

She stops moving.

Thirty-Five

Here is something they don't tell you about the desert: it's cold. Just when you think it can't get any hotter, when you feel like you might pass out from the heat—so you stop crawling, stop moving at all, and just lie down on the floor of a dry basin (like a childless injured mountain lion)—this is when it gets cold. Then you want the heat back. You curse yourself for being such an idiot, for wearing shorts in the first place. If you hadn't worn shorts, your legs wouldn't be all cut up. Your legs wouldn't be cold. But your legs are cut up and cold. Because you know nothing.

I do know one thing: I have to pee. Groaning, I crawl out of my supine position, then carefully remove my shorts and underwear so I can do it on my knees. This pee is far less triumphant than my last one (the cowboy dust-piss), and you could probably chart my desert demise through the waning glory of my pee (a whole character arc as told in urine).

"Pee is not a plot point," an editor once said to me.

I disagree. There is never enough pee in novels. We pee as much as we eat and drink, and characters are always eating and drinking—but never peeing. The pee canon. If I make it out of here alive, I think I will base the desert revelation in my novel around something having to do with pee.

I wipe with the same pissy napkin (now dry) that I've been

storing in my shorts pocket. Then I place the napkin back in the pocket and put my underwear and shorts on.

Evening has come. The clouds over the basin are turning yellow and pink; the last of the sun's white rays petering out behind the barren mountain range. It seems impossible that it could be so late, that I've been out here all day, but the clock on my phone says 5:59 (still no bars). Nature is full of things unforeseen. This is something I'm learning.

Another thing I'm learning: desert animals are nocturnal. At least, the lizard-iguana is a night-mover. In the last five minutes, I've seen more lizard-iguanas than I have in three days. They are everywhere: peeping out of cracks, out of holes, surfacing from under rocks, scuttling together, parading, baying silently like tiny dinosaurs getting ready for the moon. It's party time for the lizard-iguanas.

I take this as a sign that it's time for me to start moving again too. I don't know the migratory patterns of the childless injured mountain lion, but if she were here, I think she would agree with the lizard-iguanas: less sun means less energy expended. Be nocturnal.

But where to go?

The mountain range (where the sun is setting) is clearly west. Los Angeles is west. Best Western is west. Unfortunately, I'm not a bird. I can't just fly west. And all the nitty-gritty land stuff, the twists and turns, ridges and crests that will lead me back to anything I know are a blur of norths and easts and souths and other elusive directions. I need a route. I need a map. And I have no map (need phone reception for that). I'm lucky that I still have any battery left (16 percent).

Given these factors, I decide that west does seem best. I button my father's army jacket all the way up and pop the collar for warmth. Then I begin my crawl into the sunset.

It's a beautiful, hot lava kind of sunset: orange and purple clouds; the mountains cloaked in quiet shadow; the sun a burning fruit on the horizon altar. If I weren't on my hands and knees, crawling for my life, I might even enjoy it.

You could enjoy it now, I tell myself. *You wanted to be alone.*

But why sunset-shame myself when I'm already battered?

My body is the real problem here. If I could be bodiless—or at least, senseless—I'd be better off. So many parts of me are in pain (I didn't know there could be so many parts in pain!). I'm like an accordion of hurt! Every time I crawl, new pain notes play in different combinations: hand burns, ankle throbs; ankle throbs, knuckles sting; knuckles sting, knees ache; knees ache, hand burns; hand burns, ankle throbs. I'm a crawling, clattering one-woman band—the burning, throbbing, aching, and stinging syncopated by my gasps and sighs and moans.

To make matters worse, there's a strong wind picking up, blowing sand and pebbles in my face. I keep *fffff*ing the sand away with my lips, but more just comes. It's disheartening to be working against the wind. I debate changing directions, but the mountain range on the horizon tells me to stay the course.

The mountain range has become my ally. It's an arbitrary alliance, as I have no idea what the range is or what's on the other side. But I need something to move toward. And so this stranger is now my friend.

I do wonder whether this range is related to Red Rock Mountain, and if so, how? Are they siblings? Cousins? Enemies? Red Rock Mountain is lurking somewhere, out of sight, but it could be hiding just beyond this range. Are the mountains working in cahoots to try to destroy me? Are they laughing? Will I somehow get through this range only to be thwarted by Red Rock Mountain and regret not having followed the wind instead?

Who knows, if I see Red Rock Mountain again, I might even consider it a friend. Such is the measure of my desperation (what was only hours ago a symbol of danger, injury, lostness, is now, at least, a geographic feature I know).

Stop placing so much value on the known, I tell myself. *Fake like this is the hero's journey. It's good to get lost. Good for the soul.*

But how lost is the good amount of lost? If I die here, is that still good for the soul? Right now, my soul just feels terrified. My soul is saying, *Please! No more unknown!*

I remember once on *I Should Be Dead*, a dude said that he never really felt lost—not the whole time he was lost—because he sees all of nature as his home. I think the dude's name was Justin, and I wish I were Justin, because if I were Justin, and all of nature felt like home, then there wouldn't be such a thing as the unknown—or at least, I wouldn't be afraid of it.

But what came first: Justin being an unafraid kind of person, or Justin seeing all of nature as his home? Probably the former. And I am no Justin, not even close. I am afraid of nature. I am afraid of the unknown. I'm afraid of everything. I'm not a good faker.

Thirty-Six

I want to be unafraid. I want to be stupid and brave. I think I have the stupid part down (woman walks into desert with less than a gallon of water and doesn't tell anyone where she is going). I'd like the bravery.

The cold is a real fact now. The cold and the dark. I am moving forward in darkness, full of dread, all distant vision obscured. I can no longer see the friendly mountain range. The faraway is gone. I can see a little right in front of me by the light of my phone (battery 13 percent): some Joshua trees back on the scene; my own hand on the ground, frozen and lonely. But the rest of the world, the bigger picture, is darkness.

There are some stars but no moon. I would give a lot for a moon right now, even just a fingernail sliver to light my way. I keep banging into shrubs, scratching up my cold legs. At this point, the only direction I know is forward (and *forward* just means *onward*).

Oh, Dad. This is how I have felt all winter. This lost (and this foolish about the lostness). This feeling, and this fear of the feeling (the fear that I've done something wrong, that I wouldn't have to feel this feeling if I'd done differently, that I shouldn't feel this feeling, that the feeling is unseemly or irrational or bad or dangerous or too much, that I am all these things). So many judgments.

To have an experience, and to have a feeling about an experience, and to judge neither the feeling or the experience? That seems impossible. All feelings are not home. The inner unknown.

Are you still here, Dad, are you still on Earth? I sense that you are. I am lost. Was this how you felt in the hospital bed? Darkness all around. Your body broken and your voice like a phone that wouldn't connect. Empathy vs. compassion. Who was I to think I could hurdle the darkness when there was no reception?

The wind is angry. It blows me back. I crawl forward a few steps; then get slapped. I'm being beaten by it. When I start moving again, it's hard to control my limbs. They feel like glass. Even my bones are cold. I'm working against such wild gusts (and what am I working toward?). I feel feral. But I am not a feral creature.

I need to be buried. Under blankets. I want to be buried under blankets with heaters blasting. I don't care where they come from; just make it happen. I have to get warm. How?

I could build a fire. I could rub my friends the rocks together, somehow catch a spark. Would they spark? Would they spark for me? But what to use to catch the spark? What is there to burn?

Everything. Everything is burnable—that part is easy; everything dry. There are shrubs, and the leaves of the Joshua trees, and bits of frazzled sticks, and grasses, and hunks of petrified wood like driftwood: white and sun-bleached. It's the spark that's missing. It's the start I need.

But I have matches. Yes. Matches. The ones I put in the inner pocket of the army jacket. No cactus, no cigarettes, but matches?

I reach my hand inside the warm pocket.

Ah ha ha ha! Matches. Real matches in a cardboard book. Nine lovely, beautiful paper matches.

Now to collect something to burn. I set my phone to flashlight mode (battery 12 percent). The dying battery is troubling, but I can't worry about it. Can't worry about the wind either. Focus on two elements: fire and earth. Must collect. I am a hunter-gatherer (mostly gatherer) on my hands and knees. It's good to have a mission, like the fire is already lit. It's like scoring drugs (you're high as soon as you know you're getting them). Stay on the brink of fire. The brink of fire is better than fear of no fire.

I gather rocks: fist-size, utilitarian (less quartzy and shimmering than my small friends). I collect fourteen and set them up in a big circle. Then I dig inside the circle with my hands, scraping at the cold, gravelly sand with my fingernails. I make a firepit—a small abyss (I like that this abyss has a bottom; if only all abysses did).

I collect kindling: dry sticks, piney bark, and ghostly weeds baked to near transparency from the days of heat. I tear up chunks of brittle brush with my good hand, storing it in my jacket pockets, muling it back and forth from the pit on my hands and knees. The pile grows.

I search for fuel: wood rubble, lifeless branches and limbs, hunks of dead stump. Hauling these bigger pieces is harder. I need both hands to carry them, and so I become an upright vertebrate again—hopping on my good foot, to and from the pit.

The foraging makes me thirsty. I allow myself two rings from the water bottle (four sips). I have seven rings left (fourteen sips). The water is disappearing. I am disappearing. But fire-building is a delightful way of unbeing. At points, I am so lost in the process that I'm even pain-free.

Battery 9 percent. Need to start while I still have light. I put half the kindling pile inside the pit. Then I build a pyramid of branches and sticks. I'm amazed that I remember how to do this (I was never a good camper; only enjoyed self-soothing with marshmallows). The bigger fuel goes in crosswise, leaving lots of air holes (this I remember specifically; the holes were where the marshmallows went).

Battery 8 percent. I pick up the matchbook, nervous to try. I could easily burn through all nine.

With shaking hands, I tear off one match and strike it. A flicker comes alive. Then it vanishes. Smoke. The smell of burnt match tip. Shit. But I still have eight more matches left.

Match two. I strike it, and it lights. This time, I use my good hand as a buffer. Quickly, I cup my palm around the baby flame. The flame flickers, makes a small sound like beating wings. Then it goes out. I was right to worry about the wind.

I need stronger matches. Strike two at a time? I'm like a gambler, strategizing. Bet on two and win big or lose everything faster.

Bet on two. Have to try. I strike them both, and one match catches. It lights up its brother. I cup my hand around the double yellow flame. This time, the flame stays lit. I toss both matches into the kindling, and one stringy weed catches. For a few shining seconds, it blazes orange. Then everything goes out.

Darkness and hopelessness. Smoke smell and ashes. Weird elusive stupid laws of nature. Where is my incandescence? I need a whole hearth. I need pyrotechnics! Try again?

Try again. Double match. Strike. Light. Hand cup. Toss. Another stringy weed goes up. A stick catches on the weed, and I hold my breath. The burning stick looks like grace. Amen amen amen. Survival, baby! Then, everything out again.

This isn't working. Only three matches left. I need a stronger ignition, something faker than nature. I need a Duraflame.

I rummage through the tote for things to burn. Blueberry muffin? No. Small box of Frosted Flakes? Yes. Original bag from the Grab N' Go? Double yes. The bag is made of waxy paper (good; very un-nature).

I remove the Frosted Flakes pouch from its box (save the flakes). Then I fish the ol' piss napkin from my shorts pocket. I ball up napkin and box, stick them in the waxy bag. I roll up the bag like a log. Frosted Piss N' Go.

"Come on, matches," I say to the matches.

"Come on, Kellogg's," I say to the log.

"Come on, Best Western," I say to the second corporate sponsor of this fire (*Because We Care!*).

"Come on, god," I say to god.

I rip off two matches and strike. The flame catches quietly on the bag. It glows fluorescent green. A dark hole burns through the paper. Smoke pours out from the hole. Inside, I see the orange ear of Tony the Tiger. Sparks flutter down on the ear. The ear catches.

The box goes up blue. The log is lit inside. I hold it in the air like a lantern. The wind blows hard, but it only enlivens the flame. Tufts of chemical smoke blow into the wind. The log becomes a trash torch. Bless the synthetic! Bless this burning bush of breakfast cereal packaging.

When the log is half-engulfed, I crouch down and place the brilliant thing under the stick pyramid. The flames spread quickly. Weeds go up; branchlets go down. I stare at a colossal stump chunk and hope for a fruitful catch. The bigger wood is the lifeblood of this shrubby incandescent kingdom.

But the stump won't catch. It does nothing.

"You know you want it," I tell the stump. "Get in the mood."

A toothpick-size splinter of the stump finally lights. Then it all goes up, glowing red and gold.

Thirty-Seven

Two hours later, the thing is still ablaze. I'd call it a roaring fire. I'd call it a friend. Fragrant of pine, lamplike and comforting, I love this fire (and, like all things I love and have loved, I do not trust it not to disappear).

Maintaining a fire, I'm discovering, is like trying to maintain the perfect high. Some people reach cloud nine and then they slow down, maybe keep sipping (or smoking or snorting) periodically, but they do it slowly. For me, the perfect high is not so much about the pleasure of intoxication as about making sure that rapture doesn't go away. When I hit bliss, that's when I accelerate. It's the difference between seeking euphoria and being terrified of its loss.

Likewise, I can't stop feeding this fire. Under my anxious hand, the flames go from vigorous and steady to totally insane. There are red-hot coals—plenty of them—and they will surely last throughout the night, but I fear my friend will die without my constant attention, that I will wake up alone in the dark, freezing. I'm a neurotic pioneer, and my fire reflects this.

I toss in a few more unnecessary branches and see a strange flickering movement on one of the border rocks of the pit. Two lizard-iguanas are fucking—at least, I think that's what they're doing (one is on top of the other). It's some rigid-looking sex (and probably not the wettest), but it's romantic in the firelight.

In fact, the lizard-iguanas are moving too close to the flames for my liking. Incineration mid-copulation? Not the worst way to go, but I don't want to bear witness to their destruction. I stick out my index finger and give them a gentle shove in the other direction.

The lizard-iguanas are surprisingly light. They topple off the rock onto the sand, but they remain stuck together. They go right on humping (lizard-iguana pheromones are a powerful drug). The one on top is plumper than the one on the bottom, and its gyrations form tiny lizard-iguana claw cavities in the sand. I watch them a minute longer, then give them their privacy (if I had a tiny blanket, I'd place it over them as a conjugal gift).

The fire (and all the reptilian eros) has made me flushed. Also, light-headed. I count the ridges on the water bottle, and there are six left (twelve sips). I take two sips, then hold the bottle—cool from the night air—up to my cheek. I know that I should eat something, but the thought of putting anything not-water down my parched throat seems irritating. My choices for a midnight meal are either Frosted Flakes or one of two blueberry muffins.

I go with a muffin. The blueberries are a strange color (turquoise?), and the cakey part is unnaturally white. I stick out my tongue and place the tip on a chemical blueberry. The berry is surprisingly moist and delightful. A tiny oasis. But the cakey bread is like a sponge, and it wants to suck the last remaining moisture off my tongue. With hesitation, I take a bite.

The muffin chunk quickly turns to cement in my mouth. Nervous, I try to swallow, but it's like trying to swallow a handful of dry pills. This pill image only brings on more anxiety, because I remember (as the muffin edges past my molars, then parks itself at my pharynx) that I don't have my antidepressants. I haven't taken them since yesterday morning.

Just swallow the baked good, I tell myself. *Your only job right now is to swallow.*

I'm forced to use up four precious sips of water as a chaser.

Exhausted by this little episode (and by the day's trek, the heat of the sun, the hemorrhage of sweat, the cold of the night, the smoke in my eyes, plus—oh yes—the reality that I am injured and lost in a desert), I decide that my next move, in the hierarchy of survival needs, is to try to get some sleep.

I prepare to turn off my phone for the night, so I can preserve some battery (currently 7 percent) and possibility of reception (currently, still none) for tomorrow.

"Well," I say to the phone, "I guess this is good night."

I give the screen a dry kiss, then power her down. She gives me the apple and goes blank.

It's unsettling to be phoneless. The desert seems a thousand times darker now: a psychological darkness that my friend the fire doesn't alleviate. It's a new level of unreachability and aloneness. Just me and the universe.

Technically, it's always been just you and the universe, I say to myself.

Shut up and try to sleep, I reply.

But desert sleep—with no hotel or bungalow, no adobe or pueblo, no RV, no tent, no sleeping bag, no burrow hole—is not a sleep I've ever attempted. There's a rib cage problem and a head problem, a blanket problem and a pillow problem. There's a ground problem.

There's also the creepiness of unseen creatures—total exposure to any and all who prowl around at night: spiders and bobcats, coyotes and scorpions, bats, snakes, vultures. Childless mountain lions.

Lying down on my side on the gravelly ground, I tuck into fetal. I try to smush as much of myself as I can inside the army jacket. I get my thighs and knees in but not my calves. My feet, thankfully, are protected by sneakers.

I let my bad hand dangle over my head, abrasions in the air.

I make my good hand into a pillow, and I rest my cheek there. I feel a strange desire to lick the sand, because it is cold, and cold registers to me as wet. I position my busted ankle directly on the cold ground and use it as an ice pack.

I close my eyes. I feel like I'm falling. This is because I'm sleeping on an incline (my head facing ever-so-slightly downhill). I try to ignore the vertiginous sensation, and I'm almost successful. But just as I'm drifting off, I startle awake with a crash into nothingness. Nowheresville, California. Black Hole, USA. Metaphysical terra incognita. The vacuum.

I sit up with a jolt. This will not do. Rotating on my butt, I do a one-eighty. Then I lie back down on the stupid ground.

I return to fetal position. Wiggle myself up into the jacket. Dangle my bad hand to the wind. Transform my good hand into a pillow. Cough out some dust. Close my eyes again. Now I feel like I'm climbing up a hill. Climbing is better than falling.

Thirty-Eight

At night my dreams move eastward, and they do not slake my thirst: no fountains, hot springs, or saloons; no shady grottos; only heading ever on into the sun, a forever journey, dreams of desert in the desert.

In one dream I walk beside a wagon full of loot: gemstones, furs, fossils, minerals, ore. The wagon has a license plate. It says: 7WONDERS.

There is no horse or mule (I don't know how the wagon moves, but in the logic of dreamworld, I am unbothered by this). Likewise, I don't know who I am (trapper? Land pirate? Prospector? Not novelist), but this doesn't trouble me either. There is just a going; a doing and going without knowing or needing to know.

Up ahead in the distance, I see a campground: a small circle of cloth tents and a clay oven. I smell the aroma of burning tobacco—distinctly cigarette.

Moving closer, I see a sign overhead. The camp has a name, and the name is spelled out in bones:

CAMP MARLBORO

I do not like these bones—they look human (or if not human, then belonging to some kind of large mammal).

I want to turn around, but the wagon keeps clamoring on: rocking from side to side over a series of dunes. Several objects fall from the platform, clanking onto the sand: a rusted coffee can, a big knife with a bone handle, two fossils. I pick up the coffee can and see that it is full of more bones. The spokes of the wagon wheels are also made of bones. I too am full of bones: bone marching toward bone. Bone and bone and bone.

A vulture circles overhead: beaky and ugly. He swoops down for prey, face red like a chicken. I duck. But the vulture isn't looking for me (or any mice or vole). He wants treasure.

Pink claws outstretched, the vulture lands on the wagon platform. He uses his hooked beak as a sifting tool to find what he wants: Daniel Boone raccoon tail (no), Route 66 souvenir postcard (no), casino tokens (no), fool's gold (no), pink rock candy swizzle pop (yes).

He takes the swizzle pop in his beak and swallows it whole. I watch the candy move down his feathered throat in a long lump. Then he cranes his head off the wagon platform, and I think he is going to choke or vomit, but he doesn't do either; instead, he pecks hungrily at one of the bone spokes on a rotating wheel. He pecks with quick precision until the bone comes fully loose (an ankle bone, it looks like). I watch him fly off with the bone in his beak.

More bones tinkle to the ground. Then the wheel falls off the wagon. The wagon clambers to a stop. I stop too.

I'm scared now: frightened of all the bones on the ground, the ones jangling inside me, creepy Camp Marlboro.

"Natural to be afraid," says a familiar voice.

I look down and see beside me a bighorn sheep: the cartoon bighorn sheep I liked in childhood. The sheep is a soft cocoa color with a creamy underside, just like on the show, but his horns are curvy, ramlike, more flamboyant than they appeared on TV. He has a peaceful look on his face, eyes half-open, mouth shaped like a *W*. He nods his head gently and gazes up at me sideways.

"I don't want to be afraid," I tell him.

The sheep nuzzles his face against my leg. Despite being a cartoon, he feels like suede.

"Not wanting to be afraid always makes me more afraid," he says. "The trick, I think, is not to not want it."

"Oh," I say.

"Cigarette?" he asks.

He has two unlit cigarettes hanging out the side of his mouth.

"Sure," I say.

I take one cigarette and put it between my lips. It's very dry, no sheep saliva, and has a brown filter. I smell the comforting scent of unlit tobacco, sweet and bitter. We stand there for a while, not talking, the unlit cigarettes dangling from our mouths.

"These from Camp Marlboro?" I ask.

"Nope, never been there," he says, cigarette flapping up and down. "Probably same as here, though."

"Probably," I say.

"Bone here, bone there, bone everywhere," he says.

"Not easy being bone," I say.

He smiles as if he understands. A very compassionate (empathetic?) sheep.

"Nice to be with a smoker," he says. "No one smokes anymore."

I don't tell him that I quit.

"Probably why they changed the name of the camp," he says.

"What camp?" I ask.

"Camp Marlboro," he says.

I look up at the sign.

Now it reads: VACATIONLAND!

But the letters are still made of bone.

Thirty-Nine

I wake up and find myself in a desert. It's like waking up in the underworld: my head pressed against a sharp rock, my neck bent, blazing hot—already sweating. An odor of something burning permeates the air. Is it me?

The fire, I think. *Put the fire out.*

But the fire is already out. My pyramid of brush and sticks has long collapsed, turned to ash, and wisps of smoke pour from the coals. Good smoke. Please be a rescue signal.

No, it's not the fire making me sweat, but the sun: reinvigorated and rebounding across the sky in its mission to destroy me. Welcome to the desert! Only relentless extremes of temperature here. Freezing or scorching, that's what you get, and not a lick of shade.

In the light of day, I see only flat expanse from here to the mountain range: an ancient gold wasteland, with any and all potential shelters doomed to failure. Shrubs? Too short, can't get under them. Joshua trees? Their shadows are far too skinny. Scattered scrubby pines? Might cast good shade if I had a whole grove. It's a miracle that anything green survives this furnace at all. As for me? I'm broiling like a chicken in my army jacket.

I take off the jacket and feel the sun singe my already-peeling shoulders. I use my sunglasses as a mirror and examine my face. I look like a blood orange. Even my scalp is burnt. If I were an

157

outdoorsman, I'd judge me for not bringing a hat (I'm not an outdoorsman, and I'm already judging me).

This is punishment for something (stupidity?). Maybe I'm being tested; dark night of the soul (except it's bright day of the soul—not a cloud in the sky, unfortunately). Will there be redemption at the end of this fool's journey? The scary part is I cannot say. I don't know my character's arc. I don't control this narrative.

I imagine myself wasting away, a skeleton, all ribs—a buzzard's breakfast. It's not a nice vision board. I picture a grave in the middle of this barren terrain—a pixelated grave like in the old *Oregon Trail* computer game. That's a little better.

HERE LIES ME
WRITER

I've always liked the idea of posthumous success ("author's mysterious death in desert" can't be bad for book sales). Maybe I'll develop a lasting cult following, with fans schlepping across the desert to pay tribute at my grave (of course, they'll bring ample water). But before the posthumous surge comes a slow suffering, and I don't like that vision board either.

I examine my injuries. The skin on my palm has begun to blister over—blood blisters: three little red ghosts in a row. The ghosts remind me that this is the color inside me, and it sets me shivering. The same thing happens when I look at my thighs and see the dried blood smeared there. The scrapes are scabbing over, and they feel bumpy. I'm concerned I've got gravel lodged in there.

Then comes my ankle.

I couldn't bring myself to take off my sneaker and examine the injury last night. This was for morale reasons (didn't look; didn't happen), and also because I hoped the sneaker would create a support boot effect. But now the damage has progressed—my calf ballooning out of my sock like a thunder cloud—and I'm forced to look.

Gingerly, I remove the sneaker and the sock. It's a mess under there: my whole foot swollen up purple as a plum (if plums were made of meat instead of fruit). My ankle looks like the heart of a cadaver.

I push against the soft, spongy flesh, and feel hot pain. My teeth chatter. A wave of nausea hits, and a bitter taste fills my mouth. Quickly, I put my sock back on.

I need moisture, so I take out my trusty Best Western "canteen" and find the bottle is almost empty. Three rings (six sips, maybe). Less than nothing. I open the bottle and take two swigs, swishing the water around in my mouth for a long time before swallowing. I swear I can see the last dregs of water in the bottle evaporating. Quickly, I replace the cap. Where are Zip's alleged barrel cacti when I need them? They're in Polaroids at the front desk. That's where.

But people dig for water in deserts, don't they? I believe they call the underground water a seep (maybe a spring?). With my good hand I poke around in the top layer of gravel and sand, envisioning a fountain of water sprouting up. But all that comes is dust. I dig a few more inches into the parched earth, but nothing wet emerges (not even mud). I'm perspiring wildly, and the digging seems to only make my thirst worse. I cannot afford to waste energy.

There is only one real option available to me: get out of here now and hightail it west on hands and knees over the mean little dunes to the big brown mountain range. There will at least be shade there.

I power up my phone in preparation for the journey. 9:17 a.m. Zero bars. 4 percent battery.

Hello, is anyone there? Is anyone listening? It's me reporting live. From wherever I am.

Forty

Halfway between the firepit and the mountain range, I start negotiating with nature. I become a sort of pantheist: asking for grace from all kinds of things that cannot offer grace (which is to say, they cannot offer water): bedrock, salt deposits, boulders, flies.

"Moisten!" I command as I crawl across a dry lake bed.

The dry lake bed stays dry.

"Rain!" I say to the sky.

The sun shines on like a lamp. Nature will not comply.

Even the mountain range, my chosen destination, seems to be moving farther away. I wish I could send my spirit on ahead of me to roam the ridges, find a rope, lasso my body up to the highest peak (or, better yet, send my spirit out to find my car, drive it to me, then get the hell out of here).

I don't know if there's unexplored territory left in America, but if there is, I've found it. Since the last blue flag yesterday, I've seen no signs of human life: no indigenous ruins or hermit shed, no busted luggage or stray bandana. I'd kill for a piece of litter (also, the Pacific Ocean).

My thirst is its own plague—unrelenting—and not just one affliction, but several complex thirsts: triplet thirsts, or quadruplets, even. There's a mouth thirst and a throat thirst; a gut thirst and some strange nasal thirst I've never felt before in my life.

I want to snort water. I want to kiss water. I want to be a tortoise or a camel who BYOBs. I am lonely for water and have only water thoughts. I am now made of absence (and what is absent is water).

There are only two sips left in the Best Western bottle. I open the cap, then raise a toast to that asshole, the sun. The final drops are so precious that they even taste different, like blue heaven with a metallic essence. Holy water. I tap the empty bottle upside down in my mouth, but no rain comes.

I crawl on, scouring the landscape for a drink. Scorched shrubs begin to appear succulent to me. Pine needles: the possible source of a hidden, aqueous confection. I lick sweat off my own shoulder because I cannot afford to lose another drop. When I come upon a patch of yellow blossoms, I want to drink them all up.

The flowers are daisy-shaped specimens: lemon-yellow petals, tangerine centers, juicy green stems. They could easily be poisonous. They could kill me. But I am drooling over the tastes I imagine they possess: lemonade and orangeade, fruit punch and dandelion salad. I reach out with my good hand and pick one.

I bring the maybe-poison bloom close to my face. It's a succulent-looking risk. I part my lips, salivating wildly. But before I can put it in my mouth, I let it go.

The flower falls to the ground. I continue on my arid crawl. And it dawns on me then that I must really want to live. And it surprises me.

Forty-One

I didn't know how badly my father wanted to live until he was dying.

"He has a lot of hope for the future," said the hospital psychiatrist.

It was Consciousness One. The psychiatrist was there to do an assessment as to whether my father needed antidepressants. My sister and I voted yes. He'd needed them twenty years ago.

"Hope for the future," I said. "Really?"

I'd known my father for forty-one years. *Hope for the future* was not a phrase I would have used to describe him. Now he wasn't speaking or making eye contact. I wondered how the psychiatrist could tell anything.

"He's plucky," said the psychiatrist. "He has a lot of fight in him."

"With who?" I said to my sister. "Spectrum cable?"

I was hurt by my father's avoidance, and I'd come up with a story to make it less personal: that the accident and hospital stay had severely worsened his depression; that this decline in mental health was the cause of the lack of eye contact—and the real threat to his healing.

But the psychiatrist made me realize I'd downplayed something obvious. My father was in physical agony. It hurt him to interact. If he was fighting to live, then any engagement with the world around him would drain him of precious energy. He only seemed to be ignoring us. Really, he was using everything he had to survive. His nonresponsiveness, then, was perhaps not about resignation but its opposite.

Now I wondered whether my father—a lifelong cynic about therapy and antidepressants, who had never received any formal diagnosis of anything—ever had depression at all. Was it possible that for all these years I'd been projecting my own malady onto him?

The word *depression* is a failure. It evokes pure melancholia and excludes the constellation of other symptoms in a depressive's internal sky (mine: anxiety; self-hatred; exhaustion; doomy pain globe in chest). It's a failure, but it's all we have. So we use it. But maybe, like alcoholism, depression is ultimately self-diagnosed. Maybe we can't just slap the label on somebody else. This was the first time I considered this, and it humbled me.

I was humbled again, during Consciousness Two, by what transpired when my mother refused to take my father off life support.

After he'd coded twice, his prognosis was poor. My sister and I sat down with the doctor for a "goals of care" meeting, for which my mother was not present (she was at Bed Bath & Beyond picking up an "emergency duvet").

The doctor told my sister and me that my father's heart was only operating at 30 percent. Even if he was able to make it off the ventilator, relearn to swallow, get off the feeding tube, and go to a rehab hospital, there would still be a lot of other hurdles.

"Does my mother know this?" I asked.

My mother was my father's main medical contact. She hadn't told us any of this information.

"She does," he said. "But I don't know how well she heard it."

"So, what would you do if it was your loved one?" I asked.

This was a question suggested in the r/explainlikeimfive

subreddit by a user named salsanachos in response to the query: *How do I know when it's time to take someone off life support and what should I ask the doctors?*

"Smart question," said the doctor.

I was pleased. I wanted to be "handling" the situation well—impressing the doctor with my selflessness, wisdom, and calm.

"If it was my mother," he said, "who has some similarities to your father, in that she's in heart failure, and a smoker, and her lungs aren't great, I would take her off the ventilator and get her hospice care. But that's just me. It's a really personal decision."

I delivered the information to my mother.

"The doctor said, at the very least, we should sign a DNR. Dad has already died twice. His ribs are broken, and the CPR rebreaks them. It hurts him."

"Absolutely not," she said. "I'm not playing god like that."

"Isn't it playing god to keep him alive?" I asked.

I felt like a death pusher. But I feared that my mother's denial would cause my father suffering. She ignored me.

So I tried to ask my father what he wanted for himself. I told him that I would support whatever he chose.

"Are you tired of fighting?" I asked. "Do you want to just let go?"

My father nodded yes.

"Or do you want to try to fight and make it to rehab?" I asked.

He nodded yes again.

I did not press my mother further. But I remained inwardly convinced that we were doing the wrong thing. We were extending his death, not his life.

Then my father began to do better. Slowly, they weaned him off the ventilator, gradually lowering the pressure day by day, until one day, he was ready for a trach collar—an ugly-looking contraption, but miraculous, because it allowed him to speak to us for the first time since the accident. I had not believed I would ever hear my father's voice again.

"Dad!" said my sister. "You're like Rip Van Winkle! Tell us what you've been thinking!"

"Thinking?" he said. "I'm trying not to!"

My sister and I looked at each other. For weeks we'd been agonizing: "What do you think he's thinking about? Is he taking stock of his life? Is he sad? Is he angry? Is he full of regret? Do you think he's in hell?" But the truth was far more practical, more stoic than we could have imagined. What was he thinking about? He was trying not to.

"Dad!" I said to him gleefully. "We're going to get you to rehab! So you can make it home! You're going to make it!"

"I think so," he said casually.

Then he looked at us both and he said, "I can't believe how pretty you girls are."

He was smiling. And I realized that I had been wrong. He could make it! It was possible that he was going to make it! And my mother's denial, which I'd been so afraid would injure my father, was what had kept him alive.

When we left his room, I turned to my sister and said, "Whatever you do, never tell Dad that I thought we should pull the plug."

And we both laughed.

Forty-Two

Hello, mountain range. Hello, lifesaving shade beneath rocky overhang. Gratitude for whichever law of nature renders the sun a blockable entity. It is my new favorite law of nature.

I am sheltered by the quiet shadow of a kindly cliff face. Coolness washes over me. There's steep terrain left to climb to get to the other side of the range—to the next unknown—but I can't go anywhere until evening, when the sun dies down, and so this still canyon is my home for a while. I don't think it's even afternoon yet.

My phone is dark now. It died on the way. Now there's no chance of map or contact, and I am truly vanished—transformed by the wild and battery death into a nonentity (at least in terms of cellular communication). I don't know if the search for me has begun. I don't know if they've even thought about looking. I will know when I know, when they find me (or I find them), but until then, I could make myself crazy wondering. It has to be none of my business.

So what is my business? For one thing: rabbits. Little desert cottontails popping their heads out of holes in the dusty ground, then popping back in. There's a whole party of rabbits living right in this tiny canyon, which tells me that there must be moisture around here somewhere. Rabbits need to drink.

Maybe they've found the mythic seep or spring: a whole rabbit bar deep underground, a sweet little lair, where they are safe from vultures, hawks, and other predatory beasts; where the temperature is even cooler than up here under the overhang; where nothing turns to vapor and there is so much potable water they can stay there for days. Center-of-the-Earth Bar. Hare Central Station.

I imagine they have delicious snacks down there, delivered from above by a conga line of rabbit gatherers: chaparral toasties, Joshua tree leaf wraps, flora mille-feuille, and other vegetal delights. If I pay close attention to the comings and goings of the rabbits on the surface, I may discover which water-bearing plants are safe to eat.

But the rabbits are not in the mood to come out of their holes, or they can't come out while the sun is so high, or they refuse to come out because of me, the human interloper in their midst. Too risky. The most I get of any one rabbit is two pink ears, a velvet head, and a dark, suspicious eye, before the creature pops down again—back into its nest beneath the sun-bleached surface.

I must convince the rabbits of my good intentions. Pay my respects. Offer them gifts (which will double as bait—not to hunt the furry souls, but simply to lure them from their holes so they can show me which plants are safe to eat). What can I offer that's not already on tap at the rabbit bar? I have one and a half blueberry muffins. I have the small box of Frosted Flakes. I may want them later, but right now water is the priority. Still no appetite. Hunger eclipsed by thirst.

I begin with half a muffin. I break it up into little nuggets, then dot the crumbs Hansel and Gretel–style in a line from a burrow hole to an agave-esque plant. My plan is this: Rabbit smells muffin bait. Rabbit eats muffin bait. Rabbit craves more, and so fully emerges from hole, tempted by the farther reaches of the crumb buffet. Rabbit finishes buffet, but wants to keep eating. Rabbit is met with agave-esque plant. Rabbit then either (choose your own adventure) eats plant, and I know it's safe, or does not eat plant, and I assume it's poison.

I repeat the same method with a handful of the Frosted Flakes—snaking a trail from a different burrow hole to a patch of indigo blossoms with luscious-looking leaves. Although I haven't eaten since yesterday, I am repulsed by the flakes. But I want to gobble up the leaves.

Then I sit back on the sand and wait. I have nothing to do but wait. Minutes go by (or what I assume are minutes—without my phone, there is no way to measure time). This is the rabbit life in all its sameness.

To the rabbits, I suppose there's no such thing as sameness. For them, and their heightened olfactory consciousness, life is probably a stream of new and exciting fragrances. But for me—senses dulled by a constant deluge of opinions and judgments—every moment is a house of oppressive thoughts to be escaped. This is human life in all its strangeness.

Action at Burrow Number One. Out from the hole come two big ears, a buttermilk head, a black marble eye. Intrigued by the scent of baked goods, the rabbit's nose twitches like it's on a motor. One little paw emerges, then another. It's the cutest thing I've ever seen (and worth my desert death to watch this rabbit eat a blueberry muffin). I hold my breath, awaiting a bite. *Go on, take it, eat.* But the rabbit hesitates. Then votes against it. Paws withdraw. Ears vanish. The rabbit is gone, back into its hole with nothing.

But lo: action at Burrow Two! Another head pops up, bigger than the first. This rabbit is the color of cinnamon and sugar, a breakfast bun, primed for breakfast. The rabbit susses out the Frosted Flake bait. Its nose goes wild, like it's trying to snort cereal cocaine. The flake is just out of reach. The rabbit stretches its furry neck, and on its throat I see a beautiful marmalade-color patch. On the side of its head, one eye gives a quick blink.

Mr. Blinkers, yes, this is the rabbit's name. Mr. Blinkers seems crazier than the first rabbit (I relate). Also, more brave (I do not).

A decision is made. Air bun! With a spring, Blinkers is out of the hole: all white fur belly, tan poof tail, legs like chicken drumsticks. He moves in quickly for the flake, and *swish!* I give an inner cheer. Blinkers chews contemplatively. I can actually hear him crunching. Then, a double hop, and it's on to the second flake. *Swish!* Second flake gone: hoovered inside a little anchor-shaped mouth.

Another hop. A third flake. If Blinkers senses my presence, he gives no indication. I feel proud of my invisibility. I feel like rabbit Jane Goodall. Blinkers is getting closer to the test shrub. Soon, I will know what the rabbits know.

But the meal is interrupted by a sound: pebbles falling from the overhang. They land in the thicket beneath. Blinkers stops, hind legs contracting. He looks alert. His whiskers tremble, and he sniffs the air wildly.

Our eyes meet. I lift my good hand and whisper, "It's okay."

Blinkers bolts. On all fours he goes zigzagging back to the burrow. Then he disappears into the earth.

Forty-Three

I piss in the canyon sand. My urine is dark, amber-colored, like my father's in the bag in the hospital. I am a mammal, and mammals need water. I dip my finger in the froth and taste it. Bitter and salt-laden. I will collect it next time for drinking if I feel desperate enough, though it could be more of a hazard than a help to drink. They should teach these things in school. Forget algebra.

With my finger, I write the word HELP in the sand. I am open to help of any kind: human, animal, cosmic, divine. It's a nice word, *help*, the gentle flying *h* to ease you in, the juicy *el* sound middle, and the hard *p* that sticks the landing. It's confident, that *p*, as though through the act of asking, one will definitely get the help one needs. I feel far less confident than the *p*.

Seek and ye shall seek.

The thought occurs to me to suck on a rock—that it may produce saliva, like a piece of hard candy. I take out my friends the rocks and give a brief interview as to who is best for sucking.

"I'm translucent," says Door. "So I give off an aqueous vibration."

"I'm strawberry-esque," says Pink.

"Think of me like a geological milkshake," says The Egg.

"I'm not worth it," says Gray, always humble. "I'm flinty and tough."

I go with "geological milkshake." But The Egg is too big for my mouth, and no moisture is made (if anything, the arid rock sucks me dry like a sponge). I spit The Egg out on the sand. I don't pick it back up. I put the other rocks in my shorts pocket.

I feel irritable and despairing. I hate everything (nature especially), and I know now, I know (I couldn't know until I knew) a small taste of the frustration of my father's five-month thirst.

"Orange juice!" he begged, during one of my visits.

I told him I had no orange juice.

"Grapefruit juice!"

I told him I had no grapefruit juice.

"Water!"

I tried to explain why he couldn't have water. Not even ice chips.

"We don't know if you can swallow. We don't want you to aspirate."

"Don't be a nurse," he said.

"I'm not a nurse. I'm your daughter."

"Don't be a nurse and my daughter."

The nurse came in and gave him a swab with some balm on it to moisten his lips. He spit the balm out on the floor, disgusted.

A medical cart came rolling down the hallway. He turned to look at me.

"Hot dogs?" he asked.

It was never about me. It was his thirst, the raging thirst, which I could not overcome, though I wanted to desperately, to be stronger than thirst, bigger than hunger, more powerful than injury and illness, physical and mental; I wanted to be that powerful. The magic daughter.

Is love not that powerful?

I lift my pointer finger and write a word in the sand. I write the word LOVE. Is this the word I'm looking for? Is this what I mean?

I cross out the word LOVE and write the word IS. They are the same word, *love* and *is*, yes, *love* and *is* are the same. To be with. To be there. Of all the love languages, I think the greatest is to be there, the greatest of the languages, to be here for, to have been there with. Love.

Well, I am here, here I am: a new here in the desert, but same as all the other heres, because I am afraid, and I have always been afraid, that's how it's always been; no matter where the here, I am always afraid, and so I deflect my mind to a not-here, because the here is too scary, it hurts too much, which is why it's easier for me to be there for my sick father than my sick husband; the depth of my sick husband's here, he needs me, and the need makes it a vortex, a here I could get stuck in, trapped, while my sick father doesn't ask that I be in his here, I enter willingly, I come and go as I please, an optional here, a here where I am not even wanted half the time, a here I have to jump to, an aspirational here, which makes it more of an elsewhere.

But what about the first here? The big here? The I-exist here? For that, my father is responsible. I do not recall choosing. I did not ask for it. It wasn't even elective. He summoned, and I came.

"Come to the big here! You're coming."

Talk about stuck. And ever since, I have been resisting all the heres: the indoor heres and outdoor heres, the city heres and desert heres. I am resisting now.

But if this has always been the case, then why do I fear dying? Why am I afraid to die? How much more scary can it be? I may be on the way there now. Death. If nothing else: a reprieve from all these heres. Death. A big elsewhere. The biggest elsewhere. Unless, of course, it is another here.

Forty-Four

Later in the day, when the sun's oven begins to close up shop, the rabbits re-emerge from their holes. They are beautiful creatures: all curves, fur, and peace. I lie motionless on my stomach, good hand tucked under my chin, observing them—a posse of fourteen or so—in their rabbit dominion. They appear to be unlanguaged; at least, they produce no sounds that I can hear, no croaks or calls, yet they seem to speak to each other in different ways, through sniffing noses, angled haunches, even ear motions, and these gestures form what looks to be a shared rabbit reality.

I was wrong about the foliage. The rabbits ignore the agave-esque and indigo plants that I selected for them as test subjects earlier today, concentrating instead on the thicket of brush where the pebbles fell from the overhang (the ones that frightened Mr. Blinkers away). While the canyon floor is mostly barren, the thicket patch is ringed in green and yellow grasses. It's like a small soccer field in the middle of the sands of time. If you're in the market for grass (and the rabbits definitely are), this is the place to be.

Amongst the congregants at the grass smorgasbord, I spot three Blinkers look-alikes. I can't say for sure which one (if any) is the rabbit himself, but they make great understudies. The other rabbits range in color and size, from heather to honey, medium to small. There's one that even looks like a tween bun or, at most, a teen.

Teen Bun eats less heartily than the others. She turns up her sniffing nose at the grass (possibly the manifestation of an adolescent eating disorder, youthful rebellion, or simply a preference for different greenery). I agree that the grass looks neither succulent nor tasty, and I'm disheartened that the rabbits have chosen this vegetation to feast on. The brittle grass will do nothing to quench my thirst. I wish they'd gone with the agave.

Teen Bun is solitary within the pack: honey-brown and lithe, with intense eyes. She overlooks any peer pressure that the grazing rabbit herd may be applying, maintaining her state of indifference. I would not say she is snobby so much as independent. I admire her standards.

Then, in a rebellious move, Teen Bun gives a final sniff, turns on her hind legs, and hops away from the pack. Rogue! I follow, crawling about ten feet behind her cottontail on my hands and knees. The other rabbits pay no attention to our leaving.

I trail Teen Bun across the canyon floor. She is a precise and methodical hopper, swiftly dodging the biggest boulders and stones. I follow her over a fallen tree, then up into some rougher terrain at the base of the mountain range, where the ground is baked and splintered in hot brown shards. Her paws are better able to handle the turf than mine. By the time I reach a jutting yellow wall of rock where I saw her turn a corner, I'm far behind.

Hurriedly, I crawl around the corner of the rock wall. Then I stop cold. Behind the wall is a roofless cave: a vast atrium surrounded by weathered vermilion rock. The sun's remaining rays shine down into the magnificent chamber, filling the space with gold light, and it is here that I find not only Teen Bun, but a whole crew of teen buns partying the late afternoon away.

There are six of them: all smaller, younger, and shinier than the rabbits on the other side of the wall. I have discovered an exclusive, underage hare club: a lagomorph VIP room. I stay by the yellow wall at the entrance to the club and move no closer.

The buns are gathered together in a frenetic circle. At the center of the circle is an object of some kind. I make out a green figure eight lying flat on the ground, a piece of fallen vegetation, possibly. One of the teens stretches up on his hind legs, and I see past his furry belly that the conjoined discs are covered in herringbone-like spikes. Holy wildness! It's a cactus. Not my cactus. But a cactus!

The cactus looks to be of the prickly pear variety (beavertail, maybe). A quick glance around the atrium reveals several of the same species, still standing. But the buns have no interest in the upright cacti, going crazy instead on the busted, spikeless end of the fallen one—as though gravity, in capsizing this cactus, has peeled it open just for them.

A drizzle of cucumber-like flesh spills out from the end of the toppled vegetable. All around the dusty ground are greenish drops of moisture. There's no question that the felled succulent is a total hydration machine, and if I can get a hit of the slush, this may just be a survival story, yet.

On hands and knees, I begin to crawl toward the rabbits. Teen Bun is the first to look up. She makes a face like *You gotta be kidding.*

"I know it's embarrassing," I whisper. "At least I'm not a hunter. Or your parents."

Teen Bun is not appeased. There's hatred in her whiskers. One by one, the other rabbits look up at me in blank terror.

"I'm not going to hurt you," I say. "I only want your dinner."

How to convey to them that I'm not a predator? But I sort of am a predator. You can't steal somebody's dinner and still expect them to like you (not the first time I've grappled with this truth).

The rabbits scatter. Ears erect, kicking dust, they make for the entrance. Back to the banality of grown-ups and flavorless grass and burrows with daylight curfews. And I'm alone in Teen Bun Cavern with a cactus.

Forty-Five

The cactus supper gives me, if not a thorough quenching, enough moisture to get moving again: back on my hands and knees, crawling slowly up the mountain at twilight.

The weather is narcotic, warm with a soft breeze. The sky is a pale lavender color, and the first handful of silver stars are just appearing. Even the mountain is beautiful and easy—smooth onyx and brown clay, not too steep or crevice-y. The only inhospitable thing right now is me.

Unfortunately, the cactus has given me a stomachache. And so I am climbing the beautiful, easy mountain, in beautiful, easy weather, in severe pain—and in fear of the cause of the pain.

I'm not afraid that I ate poison. My rabbit test theory seems sound, and I imagine I'd be vomiting already if the plant were deadly. Nor am I afraid that the cactus was of the psyche-delic variety. The hippie period of my illustrious pre-sobriety reminds me that peyote buttons induce more of a punch in the abdomen, an overly full feeling (not to mention that psilocybin mushrooms always came with attendant nausea on the way to peaking).

This pain is void of nausea, fullness, or punching. It is a prickly, piercing feeling—the repeated sensation of being stung in my gut by a swarm of bees. What I fear is that I ate cactus spikes.

I was careful to avoid the spikes. First, I played succulent harmonica on the busted, spikeless edge of the cactus, sucking out the bitter innards (a taste reminiscent of a raw green pepper). Then I tried to extricate the rest of the spikes from the pads using a plastic spoon from the Grab N' Go bag and the flat edge of Door rock wielded like a knife. I even burned some of those fuckers off—using my last match to set fire to the cardboard matchbook, and then torching the cactus. Cactus flambé.

But my gut is brambly, barbed with vicious entities. I picture thousands of microscopic spikes, evil baby prickles, piercing their way into the soft tissue of my digestive organs. I think: *Fiberglass. Impalement. Hemorrhage. Infection. Staple gun. Hari-kari. Shish kebab.* The cactus giveth and the cactus taketh away.

It occurs to me that I am being punished for eating what was not mine to eat, that I must make restitution to the rabbits, not only by donating money to a desert cottontail organization (if I ever get out of this place), but by issuing an apology for harms done.

Though the rabbits aren't here with me, I feel that I can apologize anyway, that perhaps, through some energetic desert juju involving wind or mineral springs or magnetic vortices, my thoughts will carry, and so, as I crawl my way weakly up the mountain, I begin to pen a mea culpa in my mind:

> *Dear Rabbits,*
> *I'm sorry that I ate your cactus. I'm sorry that I didn't hunt or gather my own. Unfortunately, I only have one good foot left, and I could not risk a puncture wound by kicking down the standing prickly pears.*
> *Had I found a barrel cactus (the kind that Zip*

claimed were "drinkable," but would never drink because
of their protected status), I would have bashed it in
with a rock and drunk its innards, cowboy-style, leav-
ing your cactus alone. At this point, I feel that I too am
of protected status, and therefore deserving of destroy-
ing a barrel cactus (not to mention that all Zippian data
points should be considered suspect—including, now
that I think about it, the drinkability of a barrel cactus
to begin with—I wouldn't be surprised if his bad intelli-
gence ultimately led to my death—I trust you more than
I trust him).

Nonetheless, I did not find a barrel cactus. I found
what I found, and I hope, given this context, you can
forgive me.

Best wishes,
Human

The apology does nothing to soothe my pain. In my guts are
the slashes of a thousand needles. From my throat comes an
abrupt groan. From the mountain: echoes of the groan. From
the sky: falling darkness. And from the rabbits, the following
response:

Dear Human,
We are glad that you are being stabbed in the gut by
a thousand needles. Serves you right for your unkind
actions. Of course, nature doesn't work like that. Nature
is not in the business of "serving right," tit for tat, ensuring
one gets what one deserves or reaps what one sows (one
must sow for the beauty of sowing, as expectation will only
lead to disappointment). But if there were scales of natural
justice (scales you seem to believe in, but only when they're
to your benefit—after all, if you believed in a totalizing

justice, then you wouldn't eat beef jerky without fear of retribution), then good. Justice served.

> *Yours sincerely,*
> *The Rabbits*

P.S. That wasn't an apology. It was a rationalization.

My stomach is burning. My entrails are filled with fire. I'm sweating wildly, and I don't know what to do. Desperate, I try to channel the ethos of *I Should Be Dead* Justin. WWJD? But all I can visualize are his biceps and hiking boots.

Pain is nature, say the biceps.

Make the pain your home, say the boots.

I want to kill them all: Justin, both of his biceps, and the shoes. Pain is anger. Sickness is temper. I'm not stoic enough for this (or anything, really). I collapse against the mountain, press my cheek against the cool stone. In fetal position, I make a final plea to the rabbits:

> *Dear Rabbits,*
> *I was (and am) physically suffering. While the theft of your cactus may be seen as an unkind action, it was only an effort to alleviate (as anyone would!) my suffering. Please show mercy on me!*
>
> > *Best wishes,*
> > *Human*

From the mountain: only silence. From the sky: blackness. From my guts: an ominous gurgling. I get into a squat (bad ankle raised up like a stork) and pull down my shorts, but not in time for (plot point) a diarrhea monsoon. There's the thunderclap, the scorching rain, the dark puddle in the dark. The water I cannot afford to lose. The breeze on my ass, the nothing to clean myself up with. The stench. The deep emptiness.

And from the rabbits:

> *Dear Human,*
> *Not everyone who is suffering acts unkindly.*
> > *Yours sincerely,*
> > *The Rabbits*
>
> *P.S. Still not an apology.*

Forty-Six

And what of my husband's suffering?

The sufferings of the body: aching fatigue, dizziness, and every step a hill to climb. The red bloom of fever, glands swollen up purple, gnarling ache of muscles, volcanic diarrhea. The skeleton's refusal to comply.

The sufferings of the mind: isolation, grief, the destruction of a life. Fear of being left behind. The past: a ghost town. The future: terror of unknown terrors. The present a *why?*

Never once do I recall him behaving unkindly to me. Never once can I think of him snapping.

There were the moans and sighs and whines and complaints, which felt, at times, directed at me (this is what everything feels like when you take everything personally). But they were not directed at me. He never took it out on me. Never unkind.

How did he manage this? Different people have different constitutions, I suppose. But he's not so easygoing. He has anger and a temper, yelling at traffic, hating doctors, pissed at the weather, his body, his lot. Never did he withdraw from me either.

How did he remain so present? When illness had him buried. When there was no light.

It is miraculous what he has done in illness. What he has done is miraculous. If he were here with me now, I would tell him; I would say, *You are miraculous.*

Miraculous what you have done with love. Alone in your own desert. Not alone, but feeling alone, because you were with me, and I did not understand, however much I would have wanted to, however much I tried; I could not understand until I understood (and will forget again if I make it out of here alive).

Not alone. But all the while between us a great divide.

How did you do it? How did you stay kind?

Forty-Seven

I'm shaking in the dark, still some distance from the summit, the friendly mountain now grown steep and canopied by night.

My insides are empty but heavy. My arms and legs are useless sticks. The trouble is I have no fuel left in me. The trouble is I don't know my whereabouts. The trouble is I'm an idiot. I will not make it to the top of this mountain.

So this is what the end looks like. They'll find me wearing nothing but sneakers and an army jacket (shorts and underpants lost to a diarrhea monsoon; T-shirt used as toilet paper, then abandoned, man on the moon–style—a forlorn flag).

They'll find my final novel unfinished; a minor writer, a zero with good hair; small cult following fortified by legend of mysterious death. But mostly forgotten.

My wife is dead, my husband will say.

Strangely, I'm turned on by this sentiment. (Note: Cure for bed death: actual death. Post that to the subreddit: *I want my husband most when I am dead*.)

But dying still terrifies me. I need a lift.

Where is the gold rush? Where are the miners, 49ers, Mojave, Shoshone, Mormons, prospectors, rockhounds, tourists, rangers? Where's talking Elvis? Some West! Where are Jethra's aliens? If a UFO shows up, I'm open for abduction.

Do I get my own bathroom? I'll call out as I float up to the saucer.

187

Of course, the Jethra aliens will assure me, their eyes besprinkled with fake lashes. *And a free pen.*

My wife was abducted, my husband will say. *Consensually.*

This turns me on less than *my wife is dead*, though I'm not sure why. Chalk it up to the strange proclivities of the childless mountain lion.

Should the mountain lion have a baby?

I pull my arms inside the army jacket and rub my naked belly. No bump. I pet the fur on my groin, then stick my middle finger up inside. Dry as the atmosphere (she died as she lived: fingering herself in the dark with the summit maybe nearly in sight).

Arms back in sleeves, I feel around with my good hand on the mountainside. I feel for a baby in the rocks, a baby carved out of rock, a stabilizing baby, a baby to stand on, multiple babies, the Mount Rushmore of babies. What does a baby feel like? What is a baby?

I close my eyes and try to picture my sister's baby. But all I see is a glowing pink head: talking Elvis, but a baby.

"Help," I say to the baby head.

The baby head gives me a look like, *You're putting your fate in the hands of a baby?*

"Any wisdom?" I ask the baby head.

The baby head starts crying.

Then I start crying. But I cannot afford to lose the water, so I keep my lids shut and cry behind closed eyes. We cry together, my sister's baby head and I, on our protusion in the Earth's crust.

"I want to be home," I wail. "Where is home?"

How I love my faraway home. So easy to love home when I'm lost in the desert. Harder at home, when I am physically there, and so, the there becomes a here (the intolerable here, as I am not at home within myself; no, all of inner nature is not my home; how could I possibly make a home inside, what chance do I have, when a baby can't even do it?).

"Where is home?"

Through my sobs, I hear the sound of something beating gently. The fluttering of wings. I open my eyes and see an orb of shining yellow. A halo! My luminous entourage?

Spellbound, I rub my eyes. The orb solidifies to opacity. It is not a halo, but a small patch of yellow feathers. The feathers belong to a bird.

I am face-to-face with a giant yellow-bellied bird. The bird stares at me. Suddenly, I feel very calm.

I watch the bird breathing, in and out, like a balloon. It has a black chest, a black throat, and a black head. Just above its gray beak is another small streak of yellow.

Mustache Oriole!

"Well," I say to the bird.

The bird says nothing.

Gently, it extends one wing, a black wing with a white ribbon in it. A lift. And I know that the bird is my father. And I know that my father is dead.

Forty-Eight

I mount the bird like I'm mounting a horse: bad foot up and over its shiny back; good foot next. My legs flop and dangle as I try to find my balance. The bird's feathers are slippery, and I wriggle until I feel snug—tucked in safely behind the wings.

The bird starts taking me up. The sensation is one of floating heavenward, smooth and effortless. We float close to the mountainside, the stone-age façade sleek and laser cut in places, chiseled and broken in others. The mountain's mood seems to change every few feet.

A gust of wind slows us down, but it does not stop us. Our ascent is steady. We float past sand drifts, labyrinthine cracks, and aged, sideways piney trees: gravitational wonders growing horizontally off the mountain.

From where I sit, I cannot see the bird's face—only the back of its bobbing, rounded head. On the back of its neck is some kind of injury, a new scar: pink and bubblegummy. I consider diseases: avian flu, rabies. I think of my father's broken neck.

Under my weight, the scar stretches and threatens to tear. I'm scared that I'm hurting the bird.

"Is there anything I can do?" I ask.

The bird gives no response, no sign of acknowledgment. As we continue our ascent, it dawns on me that I asked this same question of my father recently.

In his hospital room, a late-evening visit during Conscious-ness Two. I was alone with him, my sister at home with her baby, my mother having already visited that morning. This was the period when my father was speaking again, the trach collar suc-cessfully implemented. But on that night, for some reason, the speaking valve was not plugged in. He could only gesture and mouth words.

"Dad," I said, as I stood by the side of his bed. "Is there any-thing I can do?"

He gave me a glance of blank confusion—such a puzzled look that I thought he was having trouble understanding what I'd said.

"Is there anything I can do for you?" I asked again, this time slower and louder.

He closed his eyes for a moment. When he opened them again, his face had changed. Now he stared at me with pointed absurdity.

Why would you ask me such a crazy question? his face seemed to be saying.

He shook his head no.

And it was a crazy question. What could I do for him, truly? There was nothing, not really, not unless I could give him what he needed most: to be fixed, healed, delivered a miracle, released from his tubes, free to drink and eat, to get out of there, to go home again. It was a crazy question. I felt ashamed for asking.

Mustache Oriole, however, seems to be making a strong recov-ery from whatever the cause of its injury. The pink scar stretches perilously, like a pair of frowning lips, but it does not tear.

In no time, we reach the top of the mountain. I'm surprised to find that the summit isn't so far from the spot where I stopped climbing below. I also discover that the summit is not a single point—no lone peak, as I'd imagined—but a lengthy rim, span-ning the whole range.

We follow the rim like a road, hovering above, tracing a path in the air. When I look down, I can see the whole range, the many buttes and vistas towering over the flatlands. I try to determine where I came from: the cracked basin where I lost faith, the cold place where I built the fire and slept, the small canyon under the overhang where I found shade. But I can't. The desert is endless, and I feel respect for every animal and plant—born here without their choosing—who make a home of this scorched terrain.

A flock of several birds fly by us. Black birds. Crows, or maybe ravens. The birds call out to my bird: sounds of greeting, warning, or, possibly, mating. But my bird does not respond, at least not in an audible way. This makes sense to me. My father was not the most talkative man.

Of course, if Carmela the psychic is right, then Mustache Oriole is not my father, not exactly, but a sign sent by my father (and/or by my luminous entourage). If Carmela is wrong, then infinite things are possible (including: that there's nothing after death and the psychic arts are a scam).

But now is not the time for existential hairsplitting. I need to hang on, because the bird is beginning to flag, sagging, dropping dangerously closer to the rugged summit ridge. We just miss hitting a patch of denuded Joshua trees, and I ask my question again:

"Is there anything I can do for you?"

This time, the bird answers me. It is not a verbal response, but a physical one. A show of energy.

We begin flying straighter, higher, with precision and vigor. The more air we get between us and the summit ridge, the more the bird shows off: speeding up, slowing down, cresting and soaring toward the starry constellations.

The bird's antics are playful yet gentle. What he seems to be saying is: *No. Nothing. There is nothing for you to do. This is what I do. This is what is done.*

I think of Jethra, the love languages, and what she said about her father. How he was who he was. *He's not going to change languages. Nobody changes languages.*

This is what it is. This is what a father does.

And it occurs to me, what my father was trying to say, that night in the hospital, the look of absurdity on his face: it was not because I was foolish, or that I should be ashamed of trying to be more powerful than I was—but that I was already doing it, I was doing it, there was nothing I could do that had not been done; and that I had been doing it since the day I was born.

Forty-Nine

Mustache Oriole and I go curling back to Earth.

When we hit the ground, I slide off the bird's slick, feathered back. My feet break my fall, and I stagger to find my footing. The pain in my bad ankle coils up my leg sharply. I shift all my weight to my good leg and stand there like a pelican, examining my surroundings.

We've landed on a narrow passage of the summit rim. On one side is a towering sandstone wall with a bevy of Joshua trees writhing from its rocks. On the other: a cliff drop of great depths. In the sky, the sun is rising gold, pink, and purple. At my feet: an abundance of multicolored stones.

"Where are we?" I ask the bird.

But the bird is no longer beside me.

I look up and see it circling the air, rising higher and higher.

"Hey!" I call out. "Dad! Don't go."

The bird flaps its beautiful wings. It looks like it's waving goodbye. Then it goes soaring off in the direction where we came from: a black cutout in the pastel horizon.

And I am alone again. Alone and stuck. The persistence of nature is deep. My body is no match for it. The range's summit (once my distant friend) now holds no hope. I can't cross over the mountain—blocked by the endless sandstone wall. I have two choices: lie down and give up or keep following the summit rim and hope that at some point the wall subsides.

I drop to my knees and prepare to crawl. My gaze lands on a big, craggy thing on the ground. An eroded log. An eroded log with a hole in it. A ghost-shaped hole. Ghost-emoji log!

Suddenly, I know where I am. At least, I think I know. Why the bird left me here. The scattered, glimmering stones. The Joshua trees springing from the mountainside. The rising sandstone wall. The steep drop on the other side. Giant cactus country!

And more than giant cactus country—this is trail country! Blue marker country! Parking lot country! The highway! The road home!

Yes, in one direction (just around the corner) we have the scene of a disappearing cactus: thirst, inferno, and sun-crazed delirium.

And in the other direction (a lot farther): water, shelter, safety, Los Angeles!

Also, grief.

Fifty

Is it bad to play along with a sick person's fantasies?

This was a question I posted to the r/deathanddying sub-reddit during Consciousness Two.

Specifically, I wrote:

My father is experiencing hospital delirium. Sometimes he thinks he's on Venice Beach. Or in his childhood bedroom. Or he confuses words based on what we say (i.e., one time I said to him, "I know you're tired of hearing us say we love you, but tough tiddlywinks" and moments later he said, "Where is the tiddlywinks letter?" to which I said, "There is no tiddlywinks letter," and he looked at me like I was an idiot and said, "Bring me the TIDDLY-WINKS letter!" and wouldn't let it go until I said, "Oh, the TIDDLYWINKS letter! Right. I'm bringing it tomorrow."). He won't let it rest until I cosign his version of reality. So I've started playing along, because it seems to give him more peace than when I correct him. But I'm wondering, is this a bad thing to do?

My question received forty-six responses, including:

The lord *detests* lying lips but he *delights* in people who are trustworthy. -Proverbs 12:22 (guitarjameson)

   Capitalists have turned politics into a hockey match where everyone is just defending their team!!! (shrimp_mittens)

   R u looking 4 a new father? I fucked your mom (Clickbait_4U)

The response I went with came from nurse_willow44, who wrote:

Yes, it's FINE to "play along" with a patient's delirium fantasies if he refuses to abandon them. I consider it the FAR GENTLER option than repeatedly correcting the patient . . . AS LONG as the fantasy is not putting him in any danger to himself, or frightening him / causing him distress, for example, a fantasy that the hospital is in a war zone and under attack, etc.

I thanked nurse_willow44, and let her know that I would continue to play along for the sake of my father's comfort.

But what I did not say was that I too found it more comfortable to play along with my father's fantasies; that, if I were honest, I would say I even preferred his hospital delirium to his hospital lucidity; that the delirium meant I could stop being self-conscious; that the pressure was off to say the perfect words, to perform perfectly (he would not remember any of it); that it was like being a sober person around drunk people (which I have never found stressful, always relaxing—more relaxing than being around sober people, who remember everything); that when he was delirious, I could be playful with him, childlike, and even creative; that I felt like we were creating our own world together—an alternate shared version of reality, where I wasn't asked to be present in the here, because, in our shared fantasy world, the here was no longer the here. It was somewhere else.

Fifty-One

One quick check. A last investigation. One final look, so that I may verify—fully, completely, now and eternally—the disappearance of my succulent friend. Then I will turn around, crawl directly to the parking lot, and it's goodbye to the desert forever. Goodbye to the dust, salt, and sweat. Goodbye to brutal distances. Goodbye to arid rimrock, waterless mazes, mournful branches, and the mass of light and heat laughing at me from space. Goodbye to my war with nature.

Just a few more yards to the cactus area (or the area formerly known as the cactus area). I'd know the way blindfolded. I could easily give a lecture on the anthropomorphized characteristics of this scenery.

First, there's the high point of the sandstone wall on the left (a primitive structure, just begging for a cave painting; my cave painting: a stick figure and the word *idiot*). On the right: the steepest drop (a word from our sponsor, gravity, about depth, powerlessness, and not being in charge). Blind man's corner (evocative of the wise seer). Turn the corner (I am neither wise nor a seer, but I am incredibly compulsive). Easy does it. Prepare to greet the nothingness.

Except there is no nothingness. Or rather, the nothingness is now a somethingness. Where before, I am sure, stood only rock and air and sky, there now stands (again!) a giant cactus.

My giant cactus.

Yep, we've got a live one, folks! Green as an olive. Tall as a crane. Fat like a concrete truck. It's statuesque and corpulent all at once: a viridian zeppelin, a brambly blimp. The grooves are grooving; the spikes are spiking; the arms are on the up and up and up. It is here, it's existent, and it's fabulous. A miracle of chlorophyll.

Still on hands and knees, I go crawl-skipping toward the colossal vegetal tower. I get up very close and conduct a thorough examination of the base. With my good hand, I sift through sand and gravel, looking for any signs that the cactus has been displaced or replaced in any way—ripped from the ground (like a tooth) or stuck back in (like a fake).

But the cactus is profoundly entrenched: rooted deep underground, anchored to the core. It's probably drinking molten lava right now. I could dig for days and not hit bottom. No, this is a binding marriage of earth and vegetable: no superficial crop circle; not some Jethran UFO or flying saucer; zero signs that indicate a departure or an arrival, no tearing or fraying, no burning or breaking; nothing reflecting a having-been-here and then a not-having-been-here and then a return.

Nothing, of course, except my memory. But this is a discrepancy that could be directional: a question of mistaken latitudes and longitudes, an error I made somehow, in thinking that the cactus was where it actually wasn't (though if that's the case, then why were the Grab N' Go bags there, right where I'd left them? And the rocks too, in a heart shape?).

It could also be a case of perceptional anomaly: scientific principles I don't understand, like metaphysics, or what Carmela said about frequency. Yes, it's possible there are millions of cacti growing all over this place that I simply cannot see, because I don't have my dial tuned correctly: CACT-FM or CCT-1060 or 101.1 The Spine! *Believe.*

But I did believe—at least, I think I believed (in spite of Zip and his stupid negations)—and where there was something, then there was nothing, and now there is something again. Something, nothing, something. With no symptoms of movement, disruption, or turmoil. Even the ground around the cactus is pristine.

There's only one sign of distress I can see, one rupture, and this is the wound on the column, the injury that was there all along (from first slit to gaping guffaw). Now the wound has shape-shifted again; no longer a jovial-looking smile, not the same slack-jawed, happy-go-lucky grin; no, the wound is worsening, or at the very least, widening. Wider and rounder. An *O* shape. A look of surprise; horror, even. A silent scream. A Munchian *O*, an *O* like: *Oh my god, I exist. Oh my god, I have to die.*

It is an *O* that looks the way I feel most of the time.

"I know," I say to the cactus. "It isn't easy."

The cactus says nothing.

"The task we've been assigned is crazy!"

I reach my good hand inside and feel around the inner rim of the wound. The edge seems to be calcifying, hardening. It's leathery. No moisture there.

"Exist! Don't exist! Frankly, I don't blame us for not being up to the task. It's frightening!"

The cactus says nothing.

"Is this why you hide?"

Fifty-Two

Inside the cylinder of the cactus, I find the familiar catacomb coolness and nave-like ribs, the lone beam of light shining in through the open wound, the holy roar of silence. The sound inside a giant cactus resembles the *whoosh* inside a seashell (that is, if one were able to fit one's whole body inside a seashell). This oceanic quality only worsens my thirst. I want to lick the wet walls.

I get down on my knees and put my face up to a succulent piece of wall between two wooden ribs. The smell of cactus meat is pungent, astringent, strong enough to make me squeamish, but I stick out the very tip of my tongue, like I'm taking the sacrament, or dropping acid. I make contact.

A bitter taste, some cocktail of bleach and horseradish, fills my senses. The nasty essence makes the prickly pear in Teen Bun Cavern seem mild in comparison. Tears come to my eyes. I blink them back and try again, but my gag reflexes revolt. I cannot stomach it.

"Please," I beg the cactus.

I don't know what I'm expecting: that by my asking, the cactus will say, *Oh, okay*, and transform its flavor from one of nail polish remover to the taste of mineral water or chocolate egg cream or a cherry Slurpee. But we don't pray to change the world (or, in this case, the cactus); we pray to change ourselves, and so I continue my supplications—my begging and protestations—in the hopes that I may alter my own perception of this bitter flavor.

"Deliver me Perrier!" I say. "Deliver me Gatorade!"

The taste is still bitter.

"Please, please, please," I moan, channeling James Brown.

A persistent sickening tang.

Still *please please*–ing, I sit down on the sandy ground, close my eyes, and lean back against the cactus wall. In the darkness, my *please*s turn to *sh-boom*s, and as I pray, I can feel the moisture of the wall coming through the army jacket: cool and comfortable.

"Sh-boom," I whisper. "Sh-boom."

The cactus juice commingles with my sweat.

"Sh-boom, sh-boom."

My pores feel awake and alert. They tingle with aliveness. Inspired, I lift up the jacket to absorb more juice, then lean back again, this time going skin to skin with the crazy vegetable. I can feel my pores open and close like tiny toothless mouths.

> *Life could be a dream.*
> There there, little pores. Latch on.
> *If I could take you up in paradise up above.*
> Rock-a-bye, pores. Take succor.
> *If you would tell me I'm the only one that you love.*
> Tipple and slurp, guzzle and gulp.
> *Life could be a dream, sweetheart.*
> Drink and drink and drink.
> *Hello, hello again. Sh-boom and hopin' we'll meet again.*

It's a titillating sensation, this osmotic experience, and it isn't just my pores that are primed for suckling. Smacking my lips, I find between them a soft, small, bell-shaped object. The bell is bitter-tasting—a different sort of bitter than the taste of the cactus, more plasticky in flavor. A rubber nipple.

Gingerly, I suckle at the nipple in my mouth. Out come several droplets of some sweet and wonderful liquid. Instinctively, I suck harder, extricating a fine, thin spray of the sugary nectar. The flavor is familiar—fruitful, plumlike—an essence I recognize, but cannot place. Greedily, I let the sweet, prune-y liquid trickle down my throat, on and on, until it comes to me what the flavor is: Dr Pepper. My father's favorite drink.

I open my eyes. Before my face is an ocean of cherry-brown-colored liquid—a contained ocean, sloshing around in a plastic bottle. At the bottom of the bottle, in a tight grip, is what looks to be a man's hand, and attached to that hand, an arm swathed in thick, midnight-blue fabric.

From where I sit, it is hard to make out precise details of the hand and arm. They are so close to my face that they appear as a blur of colors and shapes: ruddy peach skin (softly furry) and then the blue fabric. But the smells that emanate from the skin and fabric are distinct: tobacco, coins, smoke, and mulch. My father's smell. My father the father.

I gaze up, straining my eyes, trying to catch a glimpse of my father's mustached face. I want to make eye contact with him, but I can only see the auburn liquid, the plastic bottle, the hand and arm (and, much higher, the arching ceiling of the cactus). I try to tilt my head backward, but my head will not budge—blocked by something that holds it in place, something solid, yet soft. It is his chest, I think, encased in the soft, thick fabric.

I squiggle and squirm. But my father the father holds my body firmly. I am swaddled in his arm. The arm of my father the father, and his navy blue hooded sweatshirt.

"Shhh shhh shhh shhh shhh," he murmurs.

The sound of his *shhh*s resound like a harmonic mirror; a reflection of the already-oceanlike timbre inside the cactus. But where the inner cactus sound is more balanced, a sonic braid of darkness and light, my father's *shhh*s are distinctly light. They are kindly *shhh*s, patient *shhh*s, with-me-not-against-me *shhh*s. There is no correction in these *shhh*s, no discipline or shame. Only benevolent presence.

Hearing these *shhh*s, a series of words flood my mind. The words are this:

Wounded little bird. Firstborn. Why would you poke yourself with a stick? An injury is not a defect.

"Shhh shhh shhh shhh shhh," he murmurs again.

I open my mouth to speak, but I find that, for once, I cannot formulate words. I can only make noises in reply.

"Shhh-boo," I say. "Shhh-boo."

"Shhh-boo, shhh-boo," says my father the father.

No perfect words. No words at all. How strange that there is nothing I can say to make him love me more. Nothing I can say to make him love me less.

"Shhh-boo, shhh-boo."

Is there anything I can do for you?

"Shhh-boo, Shhh-boo."

No, there is nothing to be done.

Fifty-Three

But there is one thing to be done.

I stay in cobalt-blue darkness for a long time. I stay there with my eyes closed, until the *shhh*s, *sh-boom*ing, and *sh-boo*ing subside. Until the Dr Pepper runs dry. When I open my eyes, I find that it's my own fingers in my mouth, that I am suckling myself. No Dr Pepper flows from my fingertips. Only the taste of sweat.

The sound inside the cactus has changed. Gone is the oceanic hum; now there is a faint metallic buzz, like a dial tone. A dead dial tone.

I turn to my right. Beside me lies a shrunken body in a black suit. The color of the face is very white, the mouth open wide. The green eyes are open too, staring up at the sky—or where the sky would be if I were not inside a cactus. If there were a sky.

It is my father's body. My father the dead. He wears the black bar mitzvah suit and the black tie, and on his head is the white yarmulke. His feet are bare.

He is a small doll, a replica of my father. A wax figure. I reach over and touch his hair, the curls of the man. They are still the same. His mustache is there.

I don't know what part of the story this is.

The part where I bury my father?

The part where I bury my father.

I have no tools—no shovel or red sandcastle bucket, and only one good hand. I take my friends the rocks out of my pocket and examine them. Pink and Gray won't be of help (pink is too small and Gray too round). But Door is flat like a shovel. A door underground.

Using Door, I begin to dig. I dig through the uppermost crust: sand, dirt, pebbles, and stones. I dig deeper, through slab and slate and rubble. Door is a strong and hearty gravedigger, taking all these layers in stride. As for me? I am frightened.

And do I scream and cry? Do I throw dirt? Get in the hole? Of course I do. I do all of these things. It is a Bulgarian funeral.

Down, down, down. Into the earth you go. Where is the bottom? I am uncertain. But I keep digging. Digging and crying. Dig and cry. Dig and cry.

I cry until my tears fill the grave hole with water. I cry until the hole becomes a well. A private tear trove. A little seep or spring. Made by me. A small sea. I cry until the water has nowhere else to go. Sideways, then, it begins to flow. Flowing deep inside the grave hole. An underground desert river. Such is the miracle of feeling. The miracle of the Bulgarian funeral.

But my father the dead. Where is he? His waxen figure. He is no longer with me.

I search the edge of the underground river: the thick sludge and slimy herbs. I do not find him. I feel through emerald weeds and blue aloneness; gold and fool's gold; possible serpents. I do not find him.

He must still be in the cactus fortress. While I am here in the underground river. Up to my knees in the realm of feeling. Wading wearily. But wading.

Fifty-Four

A sudden splash in the heart of the river. Clear drops of water fly up like little gems. Something is bobbing under the choppy surface, something round and hairy. A bobbing head?

Another splash. Up springs a human body from the flowing water. Up like a dolphin! A body resurrected.

And it's there, in the center of the underground river, that I see him. As You do. (You, god.) Not the body of my father the dead. I see my husband the healthy.

He is young—oh god, is he young: twenty, maybe. Glamorously boyish, with eyebrows black and solemn. He wades naked in the middle of river, smooth-chested and blooming. Violet-lipped, he sets the whole river aglow with his young blood, the trail of black hair down his belly. A strong erection swelling.

He is a stranger to me, my husband the young, and this makes it easy to desire him. My husband the healthy. Hard wet health in river paradise. Vernal and flourishing.

I want to rub against him, to kiss the violet mouth: a tectonic want, very pagan. And how do I do it? How do I want my husband when he is right here? Like this. So easily.

He looks at me. I see his brown eyes shining, his cheekbones high and clean. He holds out his hand, calls out my name (he knows my name, my husband the vital). But his call is distant. He sounds so far away.

I open my mouth to speak. What I mean to say is: *I'm coming!* but the words don't come out. I can't make a sound. All this river water, but my mouth and throat so dry. Instead, I motion with my injured hand. I point to him like an arrow.

I'm coming! says my arrow-hand. *I'm coming there.*

He doesn't understand. I keep motioning, and he keeps calling, and his far-off calls are diaphonic-sounding—as though his voice has splintered in two. Neither of the two voices sounds like his voice, the husband I have known. Not as I have known him.

I close my eyes and listen carefully. The voices are so distant that they are difficult to discern, but I detect in each of them some familiar timbre. I know these voices from somewhere. One of the voices has a nasal tone, a whiny pitch. The other resonates deep and throaty, and this voice has an accent that I recognize. A Bulgarian accent.

Jethra! And Zip. They're out there, somewhere on the trail. They're searching for me.

I do not want to be found. I want to stay here forever in the underground river with my husband the healthy. And I think this is what god wants for me; yes, it's god's will, I believe, because I've heard it said that when you're in god's will you feel like you're flowing with a great river, not against it.

God's will: my husband the able-bodied. God's will: a happy feeling that comes naturally.

But if I stay here forever in the underground river with my husband the healthy, then what becomes of my husband the sick?

I try to picture him without me. I see him alone in his wheelchair, suspended in some kind of blank space. The space is white and glossy: a cheap floor, made of cheap white tiles, and the tiles stretch out around him endlessly. There are miles of tiles, square after square after square, a blank floor desert. It's overwhelming.

My husband the sick begins to wheel himself across the blank floor desert. He moves slowly, slowly, and I can feel how the wheeling tires him, how exhausted he is. All around him are red walls—not the rocky desert kind, but indoor walls; also, rows and rows of shelving. On the shelves are items for sale: packaged food and drinks, electronic appliances, even clothing. He's in a store of some kind. He's at Target.

He looks vulnerable, my husband the sick: alone in his wheelchair in this Targetian desert. I know that the energy it takes for him to propel himself defeats the purpose of the wheelchair entirely. Without me there to push him, he might as well be walking.

He turns his chair down an aisle labeled N17. It's an aisle full of housewares: curtain rods, string lights, scented candles. He stops his chair in front of the candles, picks one up and examines it. The candle is pure white in a glass jar, and on the jar are two big words printed in capital yellow letters:

LUMINOUS ENTOURAGE ™

Below these words, in smaller yellow letters, is printed:

YOUR LOVED ONES ARE WAITING.

I open my mouth to speak. What I mean to say is, *You don't need the candle. I'm right here.*

But I am in the underground river with my husband the young and healthy, and I cannot speak.

I feel the hands of my husband the sick holding on to the candle. I feel what the candle feels, the sensation of his hands: warm and human. A gentle *here.* Suddenly, he heaves a big sigh, a sigh that sets his shoulders quaking, and for the second time, I see him as You do (at Target of all places), and the sigh does not frighten or anger or annoy me. The sigh is sweet.

And I hear the sigh echoing in the underground river. It

moves like a current, rippling through the whole desert. It's in the buzz of flies and in the lizard-iguanas scuttling. It's in the beavertail cacti and prickly nettles nettling. It's in the canyons, the childless mountain lions, the bighorn sheep. It's in the snakes and humans: the shedding of skins. It's in the Gideon Bible. It's on the radio. It's on Reddit.

It is my husband's sigh. And it is the great sigh. I can hear it as I fall away in the desert. I can hear it as I almost fall away.

Fifty-Five

I leave the cactus the way I came in: out through the wound. On the trail, there's no sign of Zip or Jethra anywhere. Dizzy, feverish, and dragging, I begin to crawl the arid path in the direction of the parking lot. My muscles twitch, and my heart beats wildly.

Rounding blind man's corner, the trembling infects my whole body. My teeth and bones rattle in their sockets. It's as if my skeleton is trying to shake off my flesh. *Hurry, hurry*, say my teeth and bones. *Our big debut is coming.*

I can barely see anything. Purple spots fill my vision: floating bruises in the air. I huddle close to the sandstone wall, far from the precipice on the other side. I feel like I am getting nowhere.

But ever so faint comes the distant din of voices. Jethra and Zip? I open my clattering mouth to call for help. What comes out is just a wheezing exhale.

I have no voice. No voice, no sight, one hand. Only my hearing and my sense of smell are unimpaired. I've gone beyond emergency reserves. Now I'm on miracle reserves. Burning bush energy. I don't know what I'm burning to keep going. Light, maybe? Light and cactus spines and air.

I've become the desert. I am desert moving through desert. Desert being moved through desert. Hot desert-on-desert action. Crawling at a gallop. Fast and gone and still here. If I make it out, I want my own historic legend. Also, a ghost town and a bumper sticker (bumper sticker: I SURVIVED MYSELF).

And I might just make it out. The voices are growing louder. I'm either gaining on them, or they are yelling at each other. No, they're definitely yelling—I can discern some words now.

"Nincompoop!" (That's Jethra.)

"Not my job!" (Zip.)

"[muffle muffle] lazy American!" (Jethra.)

"[muffle] tourists [muffle]!" (Zip.)

I feel my way around gravelly clusters. I scuttle through a wash in the sand. I trapeze-crawl my broken body over cracks, fissures, and fractures. (Would it kill it to rain here for once?)

Then I clamber smack into a knotty tree trunk. My head hits the tree first, and I smell the odor of blood. Dark mysterious liquid strangeness creeps out my nostrils. Being human is so weird.

But there's good news: I can see again! The force of the impact has restored my vision. Gone are the purple air bruises. Now there's just a few-odd flashing streamers of light. And the streamers are only in my right eye. When I close that eye, I can see perfectly. Up ahead, the trail unfolds in a clean, straight shot. And what I see there: one asparagus spear; one ripe tomato.

I crawl faster. My gaze is fixed on their backs. The asparagus spear is wearing the Best Western polo shirt. The tomato is wearing some kind of skimpy halter top. I am hunter, beast, predator. They are target, mark, prey. It's hard to tell if the distance between us is closing. But I can hear them clearly now.

"We should have kept looking farther!" says Jethra. "Out past bend in trail!"

"Too hot," says Zip. "Just call the mother back and tell her we found the car in the lot."

"She could be dead right now!" says Jethra.

"Right, so let the cops deal with searching for the body," says Zip.

I try to yell to them again. Still, I have no voice. I need another signal. Something more tangible than language. I reach in my pocket. I find there my two remaining rock friends. I take up Pink into my good hand.

"Look who it is," says Pink. "Moses herself."

I hurl the rock in the direction of my failed rescuers. But Pink doesn't even travel four feet. The rock lands hopelessly on the trail in front of me. It makes no sound when it lands—not even a tinkle to alert them of my presence.

I reach in my pocket again. This time, I take out Gray.

"Not the shiniest or prettiest, but sturdy and stable," says Gray.

"You were always my favorite," I whisper-breathe back.

I wind up like a baseball pitcher. With the dregs of my life force, I heave Gray ahead. The rock sails gloriously in a silvery streak through the air. It hits Zip in the back of his blond neck.

"Ow!" cries Zip.

He spins around to look for his assailant.

I wave and half grin from the ground with my mangled hand and bloody face.

Then I pass out.

Fifty-Six

The hospital is all I dreamed it would be: heaven, just not eternal. I'm staying for twenty-four hours of observation on intravenous fluids and sugars before I am released. My room is my own, gently air-conditioned, and very clean: four white walls, cloudlike sheets, a lone window with the shade drawn to maintain separation between harsh desert sunlight and dim lighting scheme.

I'm allowed ice chips for sucking, and I tell my nurse (brown hair; not green) to keep them coming. In my mouth, the ice chips create a glass blue sensation of downhill skiing, and I'm savoring every droplet of the glimmering little icicles after so much waterless time spent in the desert.

My ankle (tibia rebreak) is swaddled in an Aircast. My hand (moderate contusion) is bandaged neatly in cotton gauze. I'm offered Percocet, but I decline anything stronger than Tylenol—explaining to the brunette nurse that I love opiates a little too deeply. All is quiet save for the scattered murmurs of doctors and nurses as they patter up and down the hall.

Then my mother arrives, and I see her drawn face in the doorway, her tense hand on the frame, and the tranquil feeling vanishes—replaced by a sinking sensation.

Quietly, I ask her when the funeral will be.

"What funeral?"

"Dad."

"Why would you say such a thing?"

She makes her way over to the bedside and gives my pillow a punitive slap.

"Bite your tongue," she says. "Don't wish his life away!"

This is how I find out that my father is still alive.

My heart becomes a fluttering wing. The air in the dim room seems to vibrate: the window shade trembles, and the white walls pulsate. In the hall, someone says the words *tissue biopsy*.

Alive.

But if my father is alive, then who sent Mustache Oriole?

"The ICU nurses are trying to get him in the best possible condition for rehab," says my mother, sitting down on the wooden chair beside the bed. "So that he'll have the best shot. I'm hoping maybe two weeks? The pants finally made it back."

"What pants?"

"The sweatpants! Amazon accepted the return, no *kinehora*. So you'll need to order them again. But don't order them yet! I'll tell you when."

Following the e-commerce memorandum, I manage to eke out bits and pieces of my rescue story.

Apparently, this morning at dawn—after two textless days—my husband broke down and called my mother, who told him that she hadn't heard from me. He then called the Best Western and was informed by Zip that I'd checked out of the hotel forty-eight hours ago.

"She went back to Los Angeles," said Zip.

"Los Angeles?"

"That's what she said."

"Did she say anything else?"

"She verbally attacked me about a cactus," said Zip. "Other than that, not really."

My husband then called the LAPD, the sheriff's department,

and the city of LA emergency management department, but none of them considered my forty-eight-hour disappearance an emergency.

"They usually turn up," said the LAPD.

My mother and my husband then left the city together in my mother's car to patrol the highways: my mother driving, and my husband (from a supine position in the back seat—"He's not a well man," says my mother, like it's new data) attempting to engage (unsuccessfully) various area hospitals, the state highway patrol, and the California missing persons hotline.

This left my mother to deal with Zip—or rather, Zip to deal with my mother, because she kept calling the front desk, and to shut her up, Zip called Jethra (on her day off) to get any further information she could provide.

It was Jethra who thought to go check for my car in the trail parking lot, and, after she found my car, who convinced Zip to come look for me on the trail. But they didn't go far enough down the trail to find me (or, it now dawns on me, to find the giant cactus where I was sheltered).

"So, who was watching the front desk?"

"What?"

"At Best Western. When Zip and Jethra were out looking for me?"

"How should I know?" asks my mother. "Like I don't have enough trouble without worrying about a front desk. I don't know why you had to come to the cockamamie desert in the first place!"

I ask her where my husband is.

"I dropped him off at the trailhead to pick up your car. We've been driving around all day. He's totally flattened. He's lying down for an hour, and then he's coming here."

"He's lying down in the car?"

"No," she says. "At Best Western."

Fifty-Seven

"Heard you got a little lost," chuckles my father, his drawn face filling the screen.

My mother is gone, back to LA. As I await my husband's arrival at the hospital, the brunette nurse has lent me an iPad from the front desk (my cracked phone is lost somewhere out on the trail). Thanks to my nurse, plus the help of Nurse Greenhair, my father and I are now connected: patient to patient, hospital to hospital. Dueling iPads.

My father has his trach collar on. The speaking valve is in. He is grayish, frail-looking, and does not appear to me to be a person near ready for rehab. But it is good to see him laughing—even weakly, with his head bolstered up against the pillow.

His mustache is growing back in. I focus on that: a familiar, furry veil of vitality over that strange, empty upper lip patch.

"Only a little lost," I tell him.

"Gotta pay attention out there!" he says. "See any bighorn sheep?"

I feel a rush of delight. He remembers.

"One," I say triumphantly.

"Think it was him?"

"Absolutely. Yes."

My nurse enters the room, carrying with her a glass vase filled with flowers. They are yellow roses—at least a dozen of them.

"These just came for you," she says.

"Wow."

She goes over to the window and opens the shade, then places the vase on the sill. I'm surprised to see that it is nighttime now, the yellow roses set against a dark sky. I hold the iPad up to show my father the flowers.

"Who from?" he asks.

"Dunno," I say. "Who knows I'm here? I've only been here a few hours."

The nurse removes a small, pink note taped to the side of the vase. She hands it to me.

We're so glad you are all right! Speedy healing.

Love,
Mary Pigg-Ratliff

Of course, MPR. I should have known. She probably ordered the flowers before I even got to the desert.

"From my UK publisher," I explain to my father. "She's quick on the draw."

"Very nice," he says.

"Yep. Now to finish writing the novel."

He nods his head feebly in agreement. But there's uncertainty in his eyes. It's not clear whether he knows what I am talking about—if he remembers that I write novels.

"Hey," he says suddenly. "I need to ask you something."

"Sure," I say.

"About last time I saw you."

I try to remember when it was that I last saw him. There was my father the dead. My father the father. Mustache Oriole. But when was the last time I saw him like this, my father the patient?

"You mean, at the hospital?" I ask him.

"No," he says.

We are both silent for a moment.

"On this thing," he says, tapping the screen with his thumbnail. "What the hell's it called?"

"FaceTime," I say.

"FaceTime," he says.

Ah yes: the botched, disconnected FaceTime. In the Wendy's parking lot. The FaceTime that launched the fight with my husband. The *GO RELAX* FaceTime.

"The last time I saw you, on FaceTime. Was there something wrong?"

I think about the Wendy's parking lot. I was in tears, desperate. I was pleading with him to open his eyes. Begging him to look at me.

"No," I say, shaking my head. "Why would anything be wrong?"

"I don't know," he says. "I've been trying to figure it out. You seemed a little—upset."

I was more than upset. I was a blubbering torrent.

"No!" I say. "I wasn't upset."

"Really? I could have sworn you seemed upset about something. Upset with me."

"Nope! Definitely not upset with you."

"Upset with yourself?"

"Nope," I say. "Zero upsetness."

"Good," he says. "Good."

Then his lips curl into a faint smile beneath the budding mustache.

"Because, you know," he says. "You are my firstborn."

Fifty-Eight

The yellow roses on the sill are beautiful. They are going crazy, crazy with life. Each petal is softly stained with a peach aureole, and this gives the impression that they are blushing: in the prime of their lives, bursting with moisture, their thorny stems full of secret water. Each stem contains a small river.

But one of the roses looks less alive than the others. It isn't just a trick of moonlight; this forlorn-looking flower—positioned on the far right—is dying. Her neck is bent. Her bloom sags on her stem. Her petals are shriveling brown and crackly. A change is occurring. The wilt has arrived.

I feel sorry for the dying rose. All this talk about loving your body as you age, but what is left for the poor flower but to crinkle and crumble, her petals falling in sheets? So sad to be the first to go, alone in her dying amongst the other flowers, who—at least for tonight—seem comfortable with time. Theirs is a false comfort (they are right behind her, next to grow old and die) but a comfort nonetheless.

But the dying rose feels otherwise.

"No," she says, without straightening her head. "It isn't sad. It's wonderful."

I ask the dying rose to please explain what's so "wonderful" about it.

"I am going to crumble," she says. "But then I'll become something else. I'm going to become a part of everything: rocks and reptiles and pinyon pines and spiders and seeds and creosote bushes and fire and rabbits and cactus flowers and bighorn sheep and even rain. There's beauty and youth for me yet."

"You have a good attitude," I tell her, crunching on a few ice chips.

"Love the unbecoming!" says the rose. "Love the becoming something else. Don't fear the unbecoming. Turn, turn, turn, and all that."

"But I do fear it," I say. "Or I forget to not be afraid. I forget god, because god is always changing. The luminous entourage—too many sources."

"Infinite," says the rose.

"I'd like one invariable god," I tell her. "One little fort of certitude inside myself. Where I can return again and again. A permanent shelter. Where I always know how to find my way back. A fort like this—it would make me a Justin!"

"Would the fort be made of certitude?" asks the rose. "Or would it only be made of words? I think that you would wake up tomorrow and see that the fort is only made of words, and you would be afraid again, and long to be unafraid. And there is no way to be unafraid, other than to let each new transformation be what it is."

"And I can't use words for that?"

"Well," says the rose. "What happens when the novel ends?"

"Which novel?"

"*Yours.*"

"Good question," I say. "Hopefully, the wife is transformed. Hopefully, she has had the kind of transformation I'm told is necessary for a successful novel, which, in this case, is the realization that love is not always a feeling, sometimes it's a verb, and that she loves her husband."

"And then?"

"Nothing. That's it. The end."

"So she disappears after the last page?" asks the rose.

"In a sense, yes."

"Transforms and then vanishes."

"Right."

"And what about you? Do you disappear?"

"No, I have to keep going."

"You keep transforming."

"Well, sometimes I transform and then forget."

"You transform and transform again. And tell me: What about life? Does that keep going?"

"It keeps going," I say. "And also, it will end."

"And also . . ." says the rose.

"That's just it! What's so frightening about existing. It keeps going and also it will end. If I could define my terror—of life and dying and loving and all of it—if I could say, *This is what it is*, I would say: *It keeps going. It keeps going and also it will end.*"

"And also . . ." says the rose.

"And also," I say slowly. "It keeps going?"

Fifty-Nine

When my husband arrives, I am in conversation with a rose.

"Hi," he says from the doorway.

I turn my head to face him. He is standing—no wheelchair—his tall body slumped against the frame for support. He looks like he could use a hospital bed.

"Hi," I say, raising my bandaged hand in a wave.

"Hope I'm not interrupting anything," he says.

"No," I say. "Please. Come sit down. The envelope."

He makes his way to the side of the bed. With a sigh, he sits down in the chair. Then he takes my good hand in his. I let him.

"Who were you talking to?" he asks.

"Just myself," I say. "You know how self-involved I can be."

I give a little laugh. But he says nothing to affirm or negate this. Quietly, he strokes my hand.

"When I was lost," I say. "Out there. I thought I found it for a second."

"Found what?"

"Compassion. Or—empathy. Whichever one where you don't have to identify—"

He opens his mouth to speak. But I hush him.

"It was more of a hypercompassion, really," I say. "Intuition. Clairvoyance—"

"Clairvoyance?"

"I had a vision. That my father was dead. I knew he was dead. I even buried him! But it was only a projection. It was about me again. Because he wasn't—he isn't—dead."

"No," says my husband. "He isn't dead."

We sit there in silence. I am aware of his breathing. Mostly, it's quiet; but on the inbreath, there is a faint hint of the wet *shhh*ing sound, barely audible, as if an imminent, future *shhh* wants to remind me that it could come on, that it might, but not yet.

"I also had a vision of you," I tell him. "This morning."

"Was I dead too?"

"No. You were alive. But I knew it wasn't clairvoyance because you were at Target. And you loathe Target."

"That's funny," he says. "I actually did go to Target this morning."

"What?"

"Your crazy mother. Made us stop at the one in the town. She's the only person I know who multitasks on a search-and-rescue mission. She just *had* to buy a hose—"

"Were you in your wheelchair?"

"No."

"Did you buy a candle?"

"No. A box of granola bars. I was starving."

"Oh."

His inhale is louder now: that thick, underwater, suffocating sound. It is a definite *shhh*, a *shhh* without a *ppp*, and maybe it's because of the lack of *ppp* that I feel no rage in response to the heavy breathing. I feel—something else?

"You must be wrecked," I say.

"I slept a little at Best Western."

"Who checked you in?"

"Somebody named Josh."

"Josh?"

"Yeah."

"I don't know a Josh. They must keep him behind the black wall for emergencies."

"What?"

"Nothing."

Shhh.

"Want to get in bed?" I ask him.

He looks at me skeptically.

"It's a little small."

"Come on," I say, patting the sheet. "Come convalesce. You can show me how it's done."

I roll over on my side. Gingerly, he climbs into the bed. We both lie sideways: me facing the window and him lying behind me, but not quite touching. I can feel his body heat in the cool room.

Outside the window, the darkness is thick with stars and possible god. Gentle clouds blow across the navy sky. The crescent moon is being nice to us, providing a soft, shared sliver of mellow light.

In the vase on the sill, the whole sky is reflected in the water. It is hard to tell, actually, whether the stars are reflected in the vase or if they are inside it. Even the moon looks like it's in the water. What is vase and what is sky?

I begin to lose myself in the depths of the vase. I see the two of us in the white bed, the bed spinning around, vertiginous, being sucked down, and I am frightened—we are both going to drown! My husband and me. In the bulb of the vase. In the vortex of the bed. In the chasm of illness. Here.

Shhh.

But he is breathing. And I am breathing. We are not inside the vase. Or, if we are inside the vase, then we are also in the sky. We're not sinking. We're flying.

231

"Like this?" I ask my husband.
I lie very still.
"Like this," he says.
He lies very still.
And we lie there. We lay and we lie. A feeling.
Nobody dies.

Acknowledgments

Deepest thanks to my agent and friend, Meredith Kaffel Simonoff; to my editor, Kara Watson (the great communicator!), Nan Graham, Katie Monaghan, Mia O'Neill, Brianna Yamashita, Emily Polson, and the whole gang at Scribner; to Alex Merto and Jaya Miceli for the dream cover; to Alexis Kirschbaum at Bloomsbury; to Karah Preiss for Kierkegaard and for your friendship; to Alex Dimitrov for the funeral; to Ryan Pfluger for the photo; to Edward Abbey and Tao Lin; to Sarah Levin Goodstine; to Nora Gonzalez; to Sharon Greene; to my mother, Linda Broder, and my sister, Hayley Broder; to Nicholas, always, for your sharp eye, warm heart, literary integrity, and for our life together; and to you, Dad.